19/32

Despatches
from the heart

An anthology of
letters from the Front

Despatches
from the heart

An anthology of letters from the Front
during the First and Second Word Wars

Edited by Annette Tapert

HAMISH HAMILTON
in association with the Imperial War Museum

First published in Great Britain 1984
by Hamish Hamilton Ltd
Garden House 57–59 Long Acre London WC2E 9JZ

Designed by Alan Hamp
Filmset in Monophoto Photina, 10 on 12pt.
Printed in England by BAS Printers Limited,
Over Wallop, Hampshire

British Library Cataloguing in Publication Data

Tapert, Annette
  Despatches from the heart.
  1. World War, 1914–1918 — Personal narratives,
  British
  I. Title
  940.4′81′41   D640.A2

  ISBN 0–241–11355–5

A royalty on each copy sold of *Despatches from the Heart*
will be donated to service charities.

Contents

A postcard written during the First World War by Edward Simpson to his wife. The reverse of the card reads: Just a card that I came across yesterday, and I hope it will be a little reminder, and give you a little comfort, when you are thinking about your loved one who, in return for your love, has offered to do whatever he can to defend and protect those that are dearest to him. The Lord give us each health, strength and patience to endure, all that is before us and soon may we meet again to part no more, Amen.

Just to say that now I'm with
The "R.A.M.C." training,
And trust that very shortly
The knowledge I am gaining
Will serve to soothe the suffering
Of some of our Soldiers brave,
And with God's help enable us
Many a life to save.

From
one of the
R.A.M.C.

Acknowledgements

This anthology would not have been possible without the help of the many regional newspapers, magazines, military journals and local radio stations who publicized my appeal for war letters. I am indebted to these publications and everyone who took the time and interest to respond to my requests.

A special thank you to the Imperial War Museum and in particular Dr. Christopher Dowling, Keeper of the Department of Museum Services.

Many of the letters I have included were selected from the outstanding collections housed in the archives at the Imperial War Museum. I wish to thank Mr. Roderick Suddaby, the Keeper of the Department of Documents, and his conscientious and courteous staff for all their assistance; also Mr. Mike Willis of the Department of Photographs for his invaluable help. It was not possible for me to deal single handedly with the mountains of correspondence I received from my public appeals. A very special thank you to Sarah Jane Learoyd for assisting me in this task and for the laborious job of deciphering and typing the war letters into legible form. Also an acknowledgement to Catherine Napier for helping with the research at the Imperial War Museum.

On a more personal note, thank you to my friends and family for their never-ending enthusiasm for the project and to my husband, Bill, for all his love and support.

The last and most important acknowledgement goes to my contributors – the true authors of this book.

A.T.

To the men who wrote these letters
and their families who waited impatiently
or apprehensively for the next letter.

'Simple men with simple motives, the chief one a
hate of injustice which grows simpler the longer we
stare at it, came out of their dreary tenements and
their tidy shops, their fields and their suburbs, and
their factories and their rookeries, and asked for the
arms of men. In a throng that was at least three
million men, the islanders went forth from their
island as simply as the mountaineers had gone
forth from their mountain, with their faces to
the dawn.'

G. K. Chesterton

Preface

The inspiration for this anthology evolved from a trip to Normandy with my aunt, Anita Bell Craig, in 1982. Normandy evoked many memories for her. She and her husband, who was an infantryman with the American Army, were married in August 1942 and three weeks later he was sent overseas, not to return until the end of the war. While listening to her reminisce, I became interested in the importance she attached to the letters he wrote to her during the war. She believed that this voluminous wartime correspondence strengthened their love and laid a strong foundation for their long and happy marriage. These were essentially love letters, but they also reflected the thoughts that passed through his mind while at the front. What fascinated me most was that my uncle was known in the family as 'a man of few words', and it struck me that his intense need for self expression was generated by the uncertainty of war. Gradually I became convinced that my aunt's collection was not unusual, that there must be people all over Britain who had letters equally stirring – packed away in attics, stored in old shoe-boxes, some unremembered and some not forgotten.

I decided to make an appeal in regional newspapers. The response from people who wanted to share their very personal letters was overwhelming and heartwarming. Their enthusiasm for the project and willingness to entrust their treasured mementos to me intensified my passion for the subject and strengthened my determination to compile this anthology.

My original intention was to collect wartime love letters but, after reading through the first flood of letters I received, I realized I could not limit the anthology. Letters written home to parents, brothers, sisters and children also had tremendous impact – and were in fact letters of love.

I have tried to give the reader a cross-section of letters written by men from all ranks of the Armed Forces. But I have made no attempt to be comprehensive, in the sense of covering all theatres of war or all types of experience, and have simply chosen – from a huge selection – those letters which spoke most directly to me. These include letters that are emotionally reflective, love letters, farewell letters, as well as material that gives vivid and descriptive accounts of life at the front and battles both famous and obscure. This last type of letter was difficult to write because of the enforcement of censorship which prevented servicemen from discussing military operations. Nevertheless, many took the risk and it is interesting to see the amount of information that managed to pass the censor's eye, especially during the First World War.

Of course, not all men wrote home to reveal their innermost thoughts, and some actually avoided them, partly because they knew the censor would be reading their private opinions, but also because they did not want to cause distress at home. For this reason I have included a few typical letters from the average 'Tommy', chosen for their plain and unadorned descriptions of life at war. The patriotism and bellicose attitudes of some of the servicemen may seem unnatural to readers in the 1980s, but they convey the genuine sentiments of their time.

It was my aim to steer away from letters written by the famous noted for their literary gifts; and to search instead for unpublished material written by ordinary people and to choose letters, not for their prose style or historical significance, but for their emotional content. None of these letters has ever been published before, with the exception that very brief extracts taken from a few of the letters in the Department of Documents at the Imperial War Museum have been quoted in other publications.

The letters have been arranged in chronological order to give the reader a sense of history: here are glimpses of two world wars seen through letters. The letters simply speak for themselves. A very brief linking text provides a few background facts, where these are available, but in many cases little is remembered and I have been unable to fill in all the details. With some of the letters, I have had difficulties in transcription. If, despite my efforts to check all material, mistakes have crept in, then I can only apologise to the writers of the letters. The original spelling remains unchanged. The letters have not been edited in any way, except that a few of them, due only to length, have not been used in full.

While compiling this anthology I was fascinated not only by what

Italian women sorting British Forces mail, Naples, 1943.

soldiers wrote, but how frequently they wrote. In 1917 an infantryman, Reg Simms, wrote home to say: 'I am just going to inform you how large my correspondence is dearest Mum, for instance in exactly twelve months I have received 167 letters besides paper and parcels and have written 242 letters in the same time.' I came across numerous collections equally prolific, from both wars. This interest in quantity led me to the Post Office Archives at Postal Headquarters, St. Martin's-le-Grand. The statistics were extraordinary: for example, in 1916 there were 5,000,000 letters despatched weekly from France and Belgium by the British Expeditionary Force to England; by 1917 there were 8,150,000. Traffic figures from World War Two were more difficult to obtain; but for the month of November 1943 in Algiers there were approximately 3·5 million airgraphs sent to the United Kingdom. Whether the content of a letter was the pouring out of human emotion or just a page about family matters, letters written and received from home were, for the soldier, the only link with the private life he had left behind.

These statistics are a useful insight into the tremendous need the serviceman had (despite newspapers and radio) to keep in touch, to escape from his surroundings or just to alleviate the boredom of long periods of waiting for something to happen. As John Harper-Nelson, a lieutenant with the Royal Fusiliers in the Second World War, wrote, 'as a further nerve-soother the local country wine that we find in each farmhouse is a great help, and also, almost more than anything else, letters from home. I suppose it's just that link with some kind of sanity that keeps us going.'

During the fifteen months of compiling this anthology I have received many fascinating letters from people who responded to my public appeals, each with their own story to tell. I think the spirit of this book, extolling the idea that the cry for self expression is greater during war than at any other time, is poignantly revealed in a comment made by Mrs. Vivienne Rawlins, the widow of one of my contributors. 'I never read my husband's letters to his mother until after his own death. I wish I had, it would have given me great insight into his character. I never knew the man who wrote those letters.' It is my belief that this book will give the reader what it gave to me – a private look into the feelings of hope, love and fear of those at war and at home.

Annette Tapert
London, 1984

THE FIRST WORLD WAR

In The Pink

So Davies wrote: "This leaves me in the pink."
Then scrawled his name: "Your loving sweetheart, Willie."
With crosses for a hug. He'd had a drink
Of rum and tea; and, though the barn was chilly,
For once his blood ran warm; he had pay to spend.
Winter was passing; soon the year would mend.

But he couldn't sleep that night; stiff in the dark
He groaned and thought of Sundays at the farm,
And how he'd go as cheerful as a lark
In his best suit, to wander arm in arm
With brown-eyed Gwen, and whisper in her ear
The simple, silly things she liked to hear.

And, then he thought: to-morrow night we trudge
Up to the trenches, and my boots are rotten.
Five miles of stodgy clay and freezing sludge,
And everything but wretchedness forgotten.
To-night he's in the pink; but soon he'll die.
And still the war goes on – he don't know why.

Siegfried Sassoon
10 February 1916

*Men of the British Expeditionary
Force arriving in France in August
1914.*

Henry Gibson joined the London Scottish as a private on the outbreak of war in 1914 and was sent to France almost immediately. He was killed at the Battle of Messines on the night of 31 October 1914.

I don't know where I am
Somewhere in France
Thursday.
(17 Sept 1914)

My Dearest Father and Mother,

Our regiment is quartered in a spacious engine shed in a little suburban looking French town. We came here from Le Havre this morning travelling all the way in fairly comfy cattle trucks. At about 10 o'clock today I caught sight of the Eifel Tower and for a long way we went along the strategic railway encircling Paris; but how far we have got to the N.S.E. or W. of Paris only God knows – as far as I am concerned. This place seems to be rather an important base, for the glorious wounded pass out from the trains in intermittent streams borne very steadily and slow. I have seen three wounded German officers, pale and somewhat bearded on the face. Some of the wounded look happy, some very sad as if they didn't know the meaning of it all. The Scots wounded are magnificent. One poor fellow with a blood stained bandage over his head and blood besotten wad on his left eye shouted to us not to get downhearted but to go in and win – he was a Gordon. A Cameron Highlander, wounded and delirious, passed from the train into the hospital shouting, 'Give me my pipes.' He evidently was a piper. But this I am giving you is only the more ghastly and glorious side of war. All the way along right from Watford through Havre and all the nameless excited little places we passed through on our way here we had a grand reception. Every station all through the night at which we stopped had prepared for us coffee or wine and bread. 'Vive l'Angleterre' was shouted incessantly. At Le Havre we had good fun singing all the good old Scottish songs – 'The Banks of Bonnie Doon', 'Kind, kind and gentle was she' and some of our chaps gave us Highland dances accompanied by the pipes. French ladies decorated our pipes with tricolour ribbon and I have a little piece pinned under my Scottish badge. We have no paper news but a presentiment haunts us all that things are well and that soon the Germans will be in a vice. The tales I hear from the wounded and from men who return from the front (I had a conversation with three men of the 12th Lancers who rode in the charge with the Scots Greys at Mons) are too detestable to mention. At any rate we are proud of our nationality, our officers and our cause and if it is fated that we enter the firing line I am sure we will do our duty. Scotland for Ever! Do write me [*Deleted by Censor*] British Expeditionary Force.

Ever Your Loving Son,

Henry

Love to all x

———

This letter of condolence was written by an officer in the 1st Battalion, King's Shropshire Light Infantry, to the widow of Company Sergeant Major John Redford. The identity of the writer is not known.

Union Castle Line
R M S CARISBROOKE CASTLE
25th October 1914

Dear Mrs. Redford,

You must I suppose have heard by now the terrible news of your poor husband's death – you will, I hope, understand how much I sympathise with you in your loss: apart from which the loss to myself and the company is very great, and he will be hard to replace. Ever since the beginning of the campaign he has been my right hand man, ready to carry out any order well, thoroughly to be depended upon and above all as cool and as brave as a man could be – I think he would have gone anywhere and taken any risk if need be – he was always an example to the men of what a soldier should be; prudent, resourceful, tactful, a good disciplinarian and his loss to me will be great –

Though the details of his death may give you pain, I cannot help telling you all that happened – on the evening of the 21st we were entrenched with the Germans also entrenched 600 yards away. On the morning of the 22nd, as soon as it was light enough to see, we found the Germans entrenching all along our line at about 100 yards. Just before dawn, they had attacked Sergeant Baker's part of the line, without success, and the German dead lay in heaps just outside their trenches, then while we were firing at them to stop their digging further their picked shots were firing at us. About 4 men in the company had been killed and your husband was walking along the trenches to see about some ammunition and was to have opened a box close to me. Just then one of the men said, "The Colour Sergeant has gone." I said "Gone where?" He replied "Killed." I looked to my left and there lying by my side was your poor husband with his skull entirely split in two by a bullet. I laid him on his back, with his head against a valise, but I saw that, although he was still convulsively breathing it was no use even bandaging the head up – one satisfaction I had; I saw where the shot came from, that is to say from a sniper in a ditch, who was every now and then showing his head enough to shoot at us. I laid myself out to get that man and at the fifth shot I got him. I did it with my legs astride across your poor husband's body, as there was no where else to stand and there was he gasping his life away. Death was of course perfectly painless and such a death as I always think most desirable. Just before he was shot, I must confess that I had been getting very excited and his last words to me were, "Don't get excited, Sir" – shortly after I was slightly wounded in the neck myself and am now on my way home to England; but I think I shall be all right again in a week or so – It is always the best people who are taken. . . . .

———

R. A. Scott Macfie joined the Liverpool Scottish as a volunteer in 1900 and was promoted to sergeant a year later. He resigned from the Battalion in 1907; but in August 1914, Scott Macfie,

Wed 23 Dec. 1914

My dear Father,

Before I forget I had better mention that some of my recent letters have not been posted on the day when they were written. Generally I have no then forty-six years of age, re-enlisted in his old unit. He went overseas with the Liverpool Scottish on 1 November 1914 having already been promoted back into his old rank. Subsequently he was appointed Company Quartermaster Sergeant of Y Company. He was awarded the Military Medal in 1916 for gallantry and in August 1917 was promoted to Regimental Quartermaster Sergeant.

time for writing until we are on the point of marching off, & then it is too late to hand letters to the censor.

We have had a very unfortunate day and I can only congratulate myself that I have got through with nothing worse than very wet and dirty clothes and curiously swelled but painless hands. We left our muddy farm at one o'clock on Monday to march to the trenches, about six or seven miles away, it being E & F Co.'s turn to go in the front firing line. We are none of us particularly well, and the whole battalion is weakened by an epidemic of diarrhoea which has been going on for several weeks. The roads were pretty bad, and as we went a pitiable number of men dropped out, unable to keep up. Among them were both my clerk and my batman, & I am now without assistance. I don't even know what has become of them.

To reach the trenches we had to end our march by a long walk across incredibly muddy fields, worked into a deep viscous sea of slime by the constant passing of troops. I was wearing new boots without nails, and my first misfortune was to fall into a deep ditch full of water, right up to the waist. A little later I tumbled on my face in the deep slime. and with a heavy pack on my back, containing two days rations in addition to my ordinary property, had some difficulty in extricating myself and regaining my balance.

The trenches turned out to be very difficult to approach even in the dark, and unfortunately there was a small but brillantly bright moon. To reach them we had to cross a very muddy field, studded with the pits shells make on explosion, pass through a gate into another field and cross it under still closer and heavier fire. At the gate the mud was 18 ins. to 2 ft deep and so sticky that it was difficult to get one's feet out, and men who fell (as many, including myself, did) had a hard struggle to regain an upright position even with assistance.

It was pretty obvious that the way to get into the trenches was to creep in as silently as possible and hope to escape the notice of the Germans, who were only 50 to 100 yards away. We were relieving a regular battalion, and their officers spoiled everything by making the first arrivals from among our men fire as fast as they could. This of course gave the game away, magnesium rockets galore went up, & a fusilade of bullets raked the area we had to cross.

My place is in the rear of the company – the last man of all. There was, of course a check at the gate and a number of men in front of me foolishly bunched themselves together in a group. Suddenly a man rolled over on the ground moaning: "My back, my back!" All the men threw themselves flat on the muddy ground, huddled in a disorderly heap. There were shell-pits full of water on each side and I could not get the men to make room for me to walk through, so I walked over the top of them. An F Co. man, member of the maxim gun team had been badly wounded in the back, apparently by an explosive bullet. While reporting the casualty at a "dug out" close by, where our officers were waiting, one of my own men was brought in similarly wounded. It was impossible to carry him, the stretchers were not with us, so they simply had to drag the poor fellow sliding over the mud. You can imagine the condition in which he arrived. It was no joke being wounded there.

One of my serjeants passed, with a bandage round his head, slightly wounded and seeking the way to the dressing station a couple of miles away.

When all the men had passed the gate the last officer and I crossed the field together. Of course I fell into a small ditch and increased again the thickness of the layer of clay that covered me, and then tripped over some loose barbed wire and made matters still worse.

There was a communicating trench from the gate to the firing trenches through which we should have been able to walk under cover. But, for want of a small pump or a simple drain, it was quite full of water. So was the first section of the firing trench, but the second bit was separated from it by a clay dam and contained only a few inches of water and mud which we baled out the next day.

R. A. Scott Macfie.

They were trenches which had been made by, and taken from, the Germans. My end the left was not bad, though the parapet, made of wet clay, allowed bullets to pass pretty freely. However, we were able to make it comparatively dry and habitable when dawn came, and if we had had materials for a fire it might have become almost comfortable though it was too small to stretch oneself in at full length. Further up the trenches were dreadfully bad – uncomfortable and insecure. Some were far too shallow, so that the men had to lie down to obtain cover; others had a foot or 18 ins of water in them; in others dead and decaying bodies had been used in building the walls. We had plenty of rum and jars of cold tea, as well as the provisions we carried in our valises, but it was impossible to send them to some of the men after daybreak – difficult even at night.

Soon messages came in that other casualties had resulted while entering the trenches. Vance, a recently promoted lance corporal, killed; an F Co. piper badly wounded; Beach, one of my men shot through the knee; etc. The stretcher-bearers arrived and I challenged them: "Halt, who goes there?" – "Liverpool Scottish stretcher-bearers" – "Is Faulkner there?" – "No" – "Citrine?" – "Yes" – "How are you doing Citrine?" "Fine, Colours!" Citrine was the sole euphonium player in the band, a good man. He wanted to go out as an ordinary private but, being intelligent, the doctor had persuaded him to be a stretcher bearer. Fifteen minutes later, they returned past me. "Well, who have you got?" – "Citrine, shot dead." It gave me a great shock.

I wanted to go up the lines to see if anything could be done for the other wounded, but the officers near me refused permission because there had been already casualties enough. I asked leave to go to headquarters or to a telephone station to try to get a stretcher to take away the wounded piper. They allowed me to go back to the gate of the field, near which were "dug outs" in which our maxim gun was kept in reserve. I reached it after falling, as usual, three times and wallowing in the mud. Luckily there was a telephone. The stretcher bearers were sent for and arrived some time before dawn. The officer refused to allow them to proceed because it was too late. The poor piper died of bleeding & exposure during the forenoon, in a trench full of water, and without anything to eat or drink, and another wounded man had to lie on his corpse. It was all rather ghastly.

We were supposed to stay in at least 2, and possibly 3 days, and at my end where we were fairly comfortable and not in serious danger, we felt fit for it. But at the other end the conditions were worse, and the officer in charge sent down messages that his men could not possibly stand another night. Arrangements were therefore made to relieve us at 1 to 2 a.m. (we were in for about 30 hours).

The Germans were waiting their opportunity, and from dusk onwards sent up periodical magnesium rockets to catch us during the change. By great care and good luck it was effected almost without their knowledge. We got out, and the others got in, with only a small addition to our casualty list. One of my serjeants was wounded in the foot, several men were scratched, etc. The total cost of this unfortunate day to us is not yet known: 4 men are certainly killed, and 8 or 9 seriously wounded. In addition we shall have a lot of rheumatism and illness. That all our clothes are soaked, that we shall not have an opportunity of drying them for weeks, that half our equipment is lost, our rifles clogged with mud, etc., is not counted seriously. Deficiencies can be indented for and replaced, and if we get rheumatism from wet boots and kilts there is a doctor to send us to hospital.

There will not be much left of the Liverpool Scottish soon. About 120-130 left the farm, belonging to the double company E & F and representing 240 who came to France. A dozen dropped out on the road, another dozen were killed and wounded and the billet in which we slept last night is now full of sick men. I do not think there are 50 men left in E Co., and it is amazing to me that I am among the survivors considering my age, infirmities, and general want of muscular power.

> Your affectionate Son
> R. A. Scott Macfie

———

Arthur Preston White served with the 1st Battalion, Northamptonshire Regiment, as a second lieutenant. Educated at Keble College, Oxford, he later made a career as a schoolmaster at Highgate School.

> 1st Bn. Northamptonshire Regt.
> 2nd Brigade 1st Division B.E.F.
> 29/3/15

My Dear Mildred,

I thank my lucky stars daily that we have no men in this company who write as many letters as you do – if we had many of your sort, the censor's life would soon be a burden to him. Heaven knows that some of them are bad enough, but you would give them all points. What you'd be like out here, with nothing to pay for postage, and unlimited time for writing, Lord only knows. You'd send some of your officers into Colney Hatch before their time.

Of course, viewed from my standpoint, you are a distinct asset, as I appreciate any sort of letter from home quite a lot. I remember once how you described Henley dining-room while a parcel was being sent off to me. Let me try a similar effort and describe how your last consignment of peppermints and gelatines. Scene, somewhere in France. Time, about 9.30,p.m. The eastern horizon is the top of a line of sand-bags, loop-holed at intervals. It is not a healthy practice to put your head up above the horizon; mixed up with the trodden slush and straw that compose the floor is the life-blood of an unfortunate man who made the experiment earlier in the day. By each loophole stands, or crouches (it depends upon the height of the sandbags and of the loop-hole at that point) a sentry, stamping his feet in the slush to keep himself warm. Occasionally there is a muffled report from one of the sentries' rifles, the sudden jerk back of his right arm and the shoulder showing that he has fired. From time to time a ricochet hums over the top of the parapet. Away on the right a bright rocket shoots up into the air from time to time, followed by a rapid burst of musketry; the Territorial regiment there are convinced that the Germans have a working party out in front. Under the parapet is a brazier filled with glowing charcoal, around the brazier, squatting on water proof sheets, are a number of rather dirty looking men. One is asleep, the remainder are discussing quietly, but very vehemently, Bombardier Wells' chance against Frank Moran. You can get two to one in five franc notes if you fancy the Bombardier. One of the party is anxious to change the subject and to impress upon the others, more recently arrived from home, that they don't know what war is and that they ought to have been at Wipers. But he is not an expert at changing conversations and his remarks gradually resolve themselves into a series of quite irrelevant interruptions.

Somewhere beyond the "horizon" a man with a remarkably fine tenor voice is singing a song. Sentimental, probably – perhaps one of the songs the four German visitors sang at Salisbury.

In the foreground, seated on a pile of sand-bags, is your excellent brother. Head gear – a sleeping helmet rolled up so as to make a kind of fez. Rather dirty face and several days' growth of beard. He wears the well-known

An artilleryman collecting the post for his battery, 1916.

old Burberry, now even more dilapidated than before. Underneath is some kind of a woolly lining. Round his neck is a revolver lanyard, connecting with the heavy Colt in his right hand Burberry-pocket. Riding breeches and leather boots that reach to the knee (as does also their mud coating) make up the rest of his visible equipment unless, indeed, you count the big portmanteau, or, to be more precise, the ingenious half-glove, half-mitten arrangements his worthy sister sent him out. At present, he is hard at work thinking of a fairly intelligent question to ask the sentry nearest the brazier, in order to get some excuse for standing near the glowing charcoal and warming himself.

A dim and indistinct shadow on the left comes nearer, and develops into the quarter-master sergeant.

"Mr. White, sir?"

"Yes".

"Your mail, sir! Brought it up with the ration party, sir!!"

"Mail? Oh, thanks very much"

The quarter-master sergeant gradually fades away into the gloom again, blocking out the light from the next brazier for a moment as he passes it. It is the last mail he will bring up to the trenches for some time, for to-morrow he is destined to stop a bullet in the thigh on his way up, thereby causing much dislocation of grub supplies. But of this everyone is naturally in blissful ignorance now.

The G.D. tries to cram his mail into his right-hand pocket, fails, because of the Colt, and tries at the left with more success. He then rises, walking with the same stamping gait that his sister favours when she makes an exit from Henley – that is, until she gets about half-way up the slopes of the hill in the Private Road. His idea is not so much to convince himself that he still retains the agility of youth, but to keep his feet warm. He soon reaches the part of the trench he wants, where the breastwork is high and there are no loop-holes. Showing lights immediately behind loop-holes is not the way to make yourself popular with the sentry who has to put his head there from time to time.

Arrived at the selected spot, the G.D. fumbles for his electric torch and makes one or two muttered observations of an uncomplimentary nature about life in general before he finds it. Now for the mail.

Letter number one comes from the Joint Scholastic Agency. There is no choking off those gentlemen – letters of explanation are of no avail, and one is forced to the conclusion that the clerks there get paid so much per hundred type-written notices. The Reverend P.E. Dagogue, of Slopton School, says the notice, has informed them that he will have a vacancy at Easter for a History and English Master etc etc the which tickles your excellent brother somewhat, for as far as he is concerned the reverend gentleman will have to keep on having a vacancy.

Now for the parcel. Letter inside – can't waste light reading it properly, have a look and stick it in pocket again. Wait until next man comes on watch. What's this? Peppermints – oh! good egg – and gelatine – thumbs up! Praise the Lord. 'Bout time I had a look at those blighters up by the maxim on the left. Exit, amid strong odour of peppermint.

There, I think I have Arnold Bennett beaten to a frazzle at making a long tale out of nothing.

We are going back into brigade reserve for a week or so to-morrow. At present we are no great way from the trenches, which we left yesterday evening. I've been letter writing almost all day.

[*Phrase heavily crossed out, with comment "Not the censor"*]. I should like one of those knife, fork and spoon combined jiggers. I lost mine when we were along Neuve Chapelle way some time ago and have ever since been carrying about a sort of sample case of Sheffield cutlery. You know what I mean; thing that folds up like a pocket knife but separates out into three parts.

I got Cecil George's letter that you sent on to me. Cecil George says the book is a big success; I wish the sales returns would bear out her statement a bit more.

Italy's intervention was a bit of a wash-out – what?

Now that you've started sending me Punch again, I have naturally started getting the blooming thing again from other sources. Try the "Passing Show". "London Opinion" is another good line – costs 1d. "Boxing" now make the following sporting offer. For 3/- down they will send their rag to any soldier or sailor for the duration of the war.

I've got a Shakespeare, that H.E.L. Dew sent me, in my valise, and I always carry about a pocket edition of the Golden Treasury. It is really amazing what a lot of time one spends in war hanging about doing nothing. There are so many objections to carting about a free library with one, that one has to make some choice of a little book that will always be fairly fresh and readable. Major Cantley has Marcus Aurelius' Meditations, the doctor has the Pickwick Papers. Chacun a son goût – what?

We have just had 100 tablets of Oxo given us, so go easy with the Lemco for a bit. Seems to me that the best way to get a thing given you free out here is to send home for it at some expense, because by the time it arrives, someone will be throwing quantities of it at you. If you didn't send home for it, you never get it issued here.

Now say I never write you a long letter and you'll be like the fellow who started the Italy rumour.

Give my love to the Henley crowd, the domestic animals and the shacks.

Yrs

Preston

———

[Undated]

Private James Crawford of the 1st Battalion, King's Own Scottish Borderers, wrote home to his employer in Banff and gave his account of the original landing at Gallipoli on 25 April 1915. The letter was later published in the local paper, the *Banffshire Journal.* James Crawford survived Gallipoli, but died on a battlefield in France in 1918. He was an old soldier, having served in the Boer War. When 1914 came, he had enlisted again despite his age, his

On the afternoon of 25th April we were transferred from our troop ship to a cruiser. We got under way after dark and the order was that no lights were to be struck. We were well treated on the battleship, the sailors doing everything for us they could, and we could only thank them. I could not tell exactly what time we got under steam as some of us were asleep when the vessel started, but the sailors told us when we were approaching the Dardanelles. We were to be at our place of landing just as day was breaking and we were up to time, but before we reached our place we were transferred from the ship to a trawler as she would draw less water and creep further in towards the shore. As we approached the coast anxious eyes were watching for the first glimpse of land, little dreaming that to many of them it would be the last day on earth.

wife's entreaties and the pangs of leaving her and three children. He said he could not conceive of any more worthwhile fate than that of fighting or dying for 'King and Country'.

Time wore on and we could hear the whispered commands of the naval officer in charge of the trawler. All at once the order was passed from one to the other to get ready for the boats 'and don't fasten your belts'. That was in case we were sunk trying to reach the beach. A sigh of relief went up as we were getting near the landing-point. Slowly day was breaking. Next came the order to the sailors who were to pull us ashore to stand by the boats and then came the other order 'Over you go'. In about five minutes we were seated in the boats, and then came a voice from the ship 'All aboard?' 'All aboard' was the answer; 'Then shove off and good luck to you men.' We were now about 40 yards from the shore and still no crack of gun, no sign of the enemy. As the sailors pulled us towards the shore, I looked round the boat. You could see the men's faces white in the grey dawn of that April morning, their eyes strained towards those cliffs where a deadly foe was waiting to hurl death on them for attempting to invade their country.

Yes, white faces there were, but not with fear. These men knew the deadly mission they were on, and were prepared to give their lives for their country. As the boats drew near the beach their was a tightening of the fingers round rifles and a mutter of 'Good luck to you mate; we'll shift them out of it' and so on. The boat on my right was the first to touch ground. Then we jumped over the side and made for the shore. Already the allied fleet was sending death and destruction amongst the Turks. I could see the "Queen Lizzie" sending huge shells plumb into one of their forces and the din was awful. At the same time, we were creeping up the steep cliffs, quite out of breath, but ready for anything. A shell burst and killed two of our fellows. We got to the top and started digging ourselves in and after a while the rifle fire started. I could see a Turkish Battery racing down to get into action but our warships had spotted them. A few shells and that battery was no more. In the meantime we were having it pretty hot with the Turks. We had poor trenches, and as a matter of fact we were

A regimental variation on the official field service post card issued to troops in the First World War.

too weak for the force the Turks put against us; but we held on all that day and all the night. We were losing heavily and no help was forthcoming. There was only one officer left in my Company. Men were falling fast and it was a case of getting wiped out or retire.

We got the order to retire, and leaving many of our brave comrades dead on the fields, we got all our wounded down to the beach and into the boats. Then we ourselves got aboard, or what was left of us. The Turks lost very heavily for they never attempted to follow us. The sailors gripped our hands and said it was terrible for they heard the rifle fire all night.

That was the part we took in the famous landing. Thank God, I came through it alright, but I would not like to go through the same thing again. The General told us next day that the Turks threw 13,000 (Thirteen thousand) against us while we were only 2,000 strong at the part we landed in.

———

Major Norman Burge, Royal Marine Light Infantry, was in command of the Royal Naval Division Cyclist Company at Gallipoli in 1915, when he wrote this letter to his mother. Later he served in France in command of the Nelson Battalion, the Royal Naval Division, and was killed at Beaumont Hamel on 13 November 1916 during the Battle of the Ancre.

On the field of battle,
Monday or Friday, dont know which
June 6, anyway [1915]

Respected Madam,
Sitting fearlessly about 200 yards from 2.000.000 bloodthirsty Turks, I take up my pen – I should say someone else's pencil (the someone being asleep) to wish you many happy returns of the day. I know it is'nt your birthday, but letters get delayed so much, this might just happen to arrive on that day. Sitting fearlessly – sorry, I find I've said that before – the sun is very hot, & I'm very thirsty. That's the chief news. The only thing there is to drink is water that comes from a nasty well, which tastes as if it had a dead mule in it (it probably has). However, we are given purifying tablets, which are very good & makes the water taste as if it had two dead mules in it. I am filthlily dirty all over & my whiskers are 2 inches long. I have'nt had my boots off for nearly a week & dont care a – for Daniel – whatever that may mean – & that's the story of the battle, I mean the last battle. Well as I said before, I'm sitting fearlessly (only thirstier still) within 100 yards of 4.000.000 Turks, I forgot to mention I've got about 6 feet of solid earth between me & them, & after all I've only got a bowing acquaintance with them. We are very polite & often bow to each other – bow pretty quick too when a bullet comes over, which must have happened twice during the last month. Battles are great fun – you always know when there's going to be a battle, because people come & tell you to get up, & bally well be smart about it too, at 2 a.m. So up you spring with a pleased smile & wring him warmly by the hand (the people) & put on everything you can find, prattling merrily all the time such as "What a delightful morning," "How nice you look, old dear," etc. Then someone strikes a match, 'cos he can't find his best girl's lock of hair to wear next to his heart (messy habit I call it) & he is gently reproved by those in authority with a smiling "Nay brother, nay, les the light attract the attention of the enemy, so please blow out that light." At least, it's something like that, only generally longer & a little louder. And then the men fall in with a certain amount of scuffling. It appeared in the early stages that everyone desired to be an even number

when they numbered off. This was because the odd numbers carried a pick or shovel as well as the ordinary gear. Now they know the value of these tools & the scuffle is to get them. Then everyone moves off & presently you get to a maze of trenches. When you get to the middle, you find a Staff Officer who says you're all wrong & you'd better go back. You argue with him, but more out of convention than anything else, 'cos he always wins. Well, you try to please him & go back, but you can't, because another battalion is coming up & the trench is very narrow. Eventually a compromise is reached. One lot (the one who lost the toss) scrabble as close to the side of the trench as they can & the others squeeze pass, scraping grooves in the stomachs of the scrabblers with stray bits of equipment which may & do happen to stick out. As soon as the General has had two bits of bacon, the battle begins. At first everyone wishes he was thinner & not quite so tall, but you forget about it after about half an hour when the rumours begin to come in. "The Turks are in full flight." "Our position is so perilous that the Staff have begun burning their maps – it's true, 'cos I saw the smoke of the fire." "The Queen Mary has just been submarined off Sedd-el-Bahr" (she's not out here, but no matter). Later, "contradict last rumour – it was the submarine which was sunk by the Tiger (she's not here either). And so on. Presently comes one bringing orders to advance & leave all superfluous gear where you are (This is just as you have opened your loathsome tin of corned beef) Off you go – hearts in your mouths & feet in your boots as they say – & do a lot of running about & get very hot. Then you go back to where your gear was & find someone's eaten all your biscuit. The great thing to do the night of the battle is to find a place where there is no field telephone. Otherwise you'll be kept up all night by some clerk (who you know by instinct is fat, clean, shaven every day & makes a fuss if dinner is late) who wants to know urgently exactly how many rounds each man has fired. If you're not very sleepy you can have some mild sport by answering either "A lot" or "A few." That is really the best opening. But if you are dog-tired – as you probably are – & can't avoid the 'phone – the best way is to get the clumsy man of the Company to walk about a bit close to it. When you have extricated him with the aid of a pair of wire cutters, you can always count on an hour or so of peace before the Signal Cr. comes along very red in the face. The next morning you think there's no more battle – 'cos you've won some trenches – when the fool of the enemy disagrees & tries to get them back again. So that there's more worry & fuss. By this time you've met lots of fellows from other regiments etc., & such a lot of tarradiddles have been swapped as to the enormous amount of ground gained by your own particular unit, that it's quite surprising to find yourself more or less in the same place as you started from. Also this is about the time you expect to get a printed sloppy effusion from the General. It will begin with "Glorious soldiers of Britain & France," so that everyone is pleased. A safe passage to bet on is "One more blow has been struck at the heart of the formidable foe," We firmly believe these speeches are kept permanently in type. However, they amuse us, & the only quarrel we have with them is that after such an intimate beginning (The glorious soldiers bit) they always seem to end up a bit curtly – no "Yours ever," I am, or anything like that. Perhaps if you're lucky, you'll presently go back to your rest camp (we hope to tonight). I've been puzzling why it's called a rest camp. The only solution I can think of is that some bullets hit the trenches & the rest come over to us. A poor joke withal, but 'twill serve & hath the merit of much truth. Well I hope you now see clearly how we fight. Send this futile effusion to anyone you like, as I dont get too much time to write letters.

Your loving Son,
Nob.

_____

In 1917 Captain Norman C. S. Down's letters from the front were collected and published in an anthology entitled *Temporary Heroes* under the name of Cecil Sommers. The letters were written to his fiancée while he was serving in France and Belgium from February 1915 to July 1916 with the 4th Battalion, Gordon Highlanders. Captain Down was severely wounded on the Somme, but by the autumn of 1917 he was sufficiently recovered to go on active service to Palestine and serve with the 14th Battalion, Black Watch. Once again his letters were gathered together and published under the title *Temporary Crusaders*.

SAME PLACE,
June 12th 1915

Cherie (French)

Still here, and no word of being relieved. That's only nineteen days that we've been in the front line without a relief, and we haven't lost more than two hundred men during the time, so we aren't doing so badly.

All the same, life's hardly worth living. From dewy dawn till the stars begin to peep the Hun shells us, shell after shell the whole day long, and we just have to sit and look pleasant. Our own artillery do their best, but all they can do is to polish their guns and think how nice it would be to have something to fire out of them. If only we could have the man here who said that there was no shortage of shells.

I'm not being very cheerful, am I, but at present I'm suffering rather badly from lack of sleep. This morning after "stand to" I told my servant to make me a cup of cocoa. Before it was ready I had fallen asleep and he had to wake me. I took the cocoa from him and tried to drink it, but it was too hot, and so I sat down and waited for it to cool. I must have fallen off again directly, as I woke up with a start to find scalding liquid tickling down my kilt and on to my bare knees. I didn't want to let my man see what a fool I had made of myself, so I raked up an old Tommy's Cooker and put a dixie of water on it. My dug-out was on fire when I woke up again, and I had to use all my remaining water to put it out. After this I gave up all idea of a hot drink and went to sleep on the sopping floor of the dug-out. Five or six hours later a small earthquake roused me to the fact that all around me was dark. This was astonishing for midday in June. A shell had closed up the dug-out door, an ungentlemanly thing to do, but better perhaps than coming in through the door. When my men dug me out they told me that this sort of thing had been going on for over an hour, and that they had retired to the far end of the trench, and had wondered why I didn't do likewise. . . .

*

Later. – I've been hit, Phyllis, and am feeling a regular wounded 'ero. I was walking along the trench when there was a bang, and I was thrown forward on to my face. "You're hit, sir, hit in the back," said one of my men, and with a breathless haste my tunic and shirt was torn off, to disclose a shrapnel ball clinging lovingly to my spine in the midst of a huge bruise. The skin had just been scratched. Oh, I was sick, I had fully expected a nice cushy one, and a month down the line, with perhaps a fortnight's sick leave in England to top up with, and then to find it was the merest scratch. Oh, it was cruel. However, the news got round, and I had a message

A corporal of the 10th Battalion, Gordon Highlanders, seizes a moment to write a letter home. Western Front, 1917.

from battalion H.Q. asking whether they should send along a stretcher! And when I went down to the dressing station to get some iodine put on the wound the M.O. turned round to the orderly and said, "Just put some iodine on this officer's wound, will you. You'll find it if you look long enough". That put the lid on it. No more wounds for me.

Till next time,
Your wounded hero,
THOMAS

Cyril Rawlins left for France in May 1915 and served as the Transport Officer of the 1st Battalion, Welsh Regiment. The letter is to his father. In October 1915 he was hit by a bridge when travelling on top of a train. He received a fractured skull from the accident and was invalided home and discharged.

August 15, 1915

Dear Goss,

How my heart ached when I pulled out your photo of Pottal Corner, that sweet spot in God's own country looking just as I have so many times seen it, the long dipping road to Penbridge and far in the distance the blue dome of the Wrekin. How it brings back memories of the time before the war, when the world was happy and careless: the Golden Age: a summer Sunday afternoon, and I with my cycle, and some food in my saddle bag, passing this spot, cutting down through the cool perfumed plantations, after the arduous climb up lovely Penbridge Bank, no sound but the drone of the bees in the heather and the whirr of the grouse: stopping now often to admire the distant view over the high land beyond Bowley! Swooping down the long grade into sleepy little Penbridge. Gailey; the long blue granite stretches of my favorite Watling Street: uphill and down dale on the whirring "wheel". Ivetsey Bank, with Boscobel away in the trees; Weston-under-Lizard, with its comfortable, respectable "model village" air, all shaded by the tall elm trees behind the grey stone wall of the Park: a drink at the pump there; then another few miles and turn left by the "Fox & Hounds", with its old bow windows bulging invitingly onto the road; up the verdant lane and across the main road: Haughton village, the "Mount", and a cordial welcome from the Osbornes: Wilfred and Harry, pipe in mouth, lounging in deck chairs, and the old man pottering round looking at his flower beds. Then, dusk and the return: a clear starry sky, and a young moon: inky shadows under the trees: rustics and courting couples strolling home: voices and subdued laughter from the roadside. The musical clangour of cycle bells: cars with their glaring eyes swishing past, the red tail lamp growing smaller and smaller in the distance: always the deep weird thrumming of the wires, a sound which has always been for me part of the Call of the Road: (I would think, as I sped along, of all the people which have passed and all the various traffic which has rolled along that Road since the Legions, swinging along at their steady three miles an hour, through the virgin forest, going north to fight the Picts, from Anderidor on the Sussex coast to Hunnum on the Wall, singing the soldier songs of their day.) Then, having threaded the dusky lanes by Bedwall, over the backbone of the chase, the drop into Milford, and the run home over the Satnall Hills. Wolseley Bridge: (I can smell the sweet rotten river-smell where the Trent bends in to the road, under the high red banks). Finally home: the little town, already asleep at eleven o'clock: the front door rattles as I enter, with its dear old Jerry-built rattle, and you call from above in an affrighted voice "Is that you, Cyril?" and I don't answer for a few seconds, to rile you; and you come down and warn me what a dangerous thing to do, and what you *might* do thinking it was a burglar!! I light the pantry gas, and on the stone find some little dainty or a half chicken for supper; I eat this slowly, going over in my mind my day's doings, and thinking what a grand time I've had, and wishing tomorrow was another Sunday, instead of Monday, and you are going to Liverpool: having suggested the advisibility of my visiting Walsall, by some after lunch train. (I forget the *exact* time!) As I go upstairs the town hall strikes midnight.

How true it is that one never values anything properly until one has lost it!! My home, and the little town, and my Chase, and all the things I had, and never appreciated, and sometimes cursed: how dear they have become!

One does not often think about these things: one is too busy, and warfare hardens a man, but now and then some little thing stirs the chords of memory and affection like nothing else, and your soul sickens for the old days: and your whole being cries out passionately for life to be spared to return to the things you love, and your home-place, and the people who are waiting there for you.

That is what your postcard of Pottal Corner has meant to me today.

Your Son.

Cyril Rawlins.

Arthur De Salis Hadow was commissioned into the Yorkshire Regiment (The Green Howards) in 1878 and served with them for thirty-two years, attaining the rank of colonel. He was fifty-six and retired from the Army when he volunteered for service on the outbreak of war. In October 1914 he took command of the 10th Battalion which crossed to France eleven months later. This set of letters to his wife was written in a space of three days. The first – a farewell letter written on the eve of the Battle of Loos. The second – the next morning while waiting for orders to move up to the front line trenches. The third – the most immediate – on the battlefield of Loos less than an hour before Colonel Hadow lead the attack by his Battalion on Hill 70, where he was killed.

24th September, 1915

My very dearest Maude,
I expect that before you get this letter we will most probably be in the thick of it and what happens then no one can foretell. We move from here tonight and shall bivouac just off the road and not far behind the firing line. The men will have nothing but their overcoats, so I fear they will feel the cold. The bombardment which is continuous will go on til some time tomorrow (I don't know when). Two Army Corps will then assault and if successful our Corps will go through the middle. It will be a gigantic battle and many will not come out safe and sound. We are going to use every kind of thing to make it unpleasant for the Germans and the Division will probably go into action wearing our smoke helmets. It is curious after having failed to see anything of active service all the years I was in the Army that my first experience should be such a big thing as this, the point we shall have to make for is 96th on the list I am sending you by this post. I know full well I shall be in God's hands. I trust I may do my duty as I ought to do and if it is fated I am to die, I feel I shall have fallen doing the right thing and that I shall be allowed to join Gerry* in Heaven. I think it right to look things squarely in the face, though naturally I hope I may come safely through and that we shall all spend a good many happy years together.

I was so glad I got the little photo case this morning, I shall carry it with me always. I feel very anxious about you dear ones, what with heavy taxes and the cost of living so increased, you will find it very hard to live with any comfort. All my securities are at Holst's, Mr. Quinten will manage all that sort of thing for you and I am sure Frank will give you a helpful hand. I will try and write again tomorrow, but may not be able to find time. May God bless and keep you well,

Your very loving Arthur.

————

25th September, 1915 9.15 am.

My very dearest Maude,
I wrote a letter to Daphne earlier this morning as I wanted to write to each of you and let you know how often I have been thinking of you all. I am now at Brigade Headquarters with the other CO's waiting for orders. Two further reports have come in since I have finished Daphne's everything so far is going splendidly. I expect we shall shortly get orders to move up to our first line trenches in readiness to go further on. We have taken the German front line of trenches and we are up to their second line. We are eagerly waiting news of what the French are doing. I want to see all our cavalry move out to the front – 9:45 – The order has come for our Brigade to move at once. Will write again if I can. God bless you all, Your loving Arthur.

————

*His son, who had been killed in France earlier in 1915.

26th September, 1915.

My dear Maude,

I wonder if I shall ever finish this or if whether this morning is my last on earth. We have had a very terrible time during the last 24 hours and in half an hour have to make another attack with what I've got of my Battalion left with me, only just over 400. The rest are not all casualties though we've already had a good many. The men are scattered all over the place. After I had written to you yesterday we marched up to firing line, or rather just behind it and halted. From the reports which had come in it looked as if we should have an easy task before us. About 2 pm my Brigade was ordered to reinforce another Division which was said to have taken and were holding a hill called 70. As we were moving towards it, we suddenly came under shell fire and later by concealed machine gun and snipers. The firing was pretty heavy and we lost a number of officers and men. We got up on a hill where we found a portion of two London regiments and as it was then getting dark we started to dig ourselves in. The Germans were shelling at us all night but did no damage. About 2:30 am they advanced to attack us but our rifles and machine guns drove them back three times and I fancy did considerable execution. About 3 we were ordered to move to another place in order to assist in the attack on Hill 70 this morning. It had been a very sharp experience for men who were under fire for the first time and Dent and I had some trouble getting the men together. By the way Dent has behaved most gallantly and worked so hard. We got to the place we were told and laid down in a field where we shortly came under shell fire. I was so tired that I slept thinking we were going to have no trouble. I hadn't even taken my coat off my saddle. It rained hard all the afternoon and again at night so everybody got very wet. I found a man's overcoat lying about which I put on and was most thankful for we moved back from the field as two men were hit by shells and I found a covered place with a German gun in it. There we made some soup. It was the first food bar two or three small biscuits and a bit of chocolate that I had had for 24 hours. Oh war like this is very very terrible, I have been preserved so far, but it seemed a marvel how I did and now we've got to go through it again. The German Infantry is no good—it's their artillery, machine guns and snipers. We are just off. Goodbye with love.

    Your Arthur.

———

Lance Corporal Reuben Elliott was serving in France with the 9th Battalion, East Surrey Regiment, when he wrote this letter home, just after Christmas.

L/Cpl. L. Elliott 1594
9 Batt. E. Surrey Regt.
Transport
B.E.F.
27.12.15

Dear Mum and Dad,

Xmas has passed once again & I was thinking of you all at home. Well, how did you spend your Xmas? Very happy & cheerful I hope. Well Mum & Dad I will try and relate my little Xmas time. I was on the go from 6 o'clock in the morning getting the dinner ready for the boys, we had chicken for dinner & potatoes and Xmas pudding, we decorated the cafe inside & out and it looked like Xmas at home, we borrowed a long table & forms, plates, knifes & forks etc. and sat down to dinner in style, the officers brought us a barrel of Beer, and bottles of Rum and they also sat down to dinner with us. We all (NCOs) gave a toast to the officers & they returned, and the boys stood up and sang "He's a jolly good fellow" and we all spent a very happy Xmas under the conditions, and finished up at 10 o'clock. Then I went to bed and had a quiet smoke and I could imagine you all at home and sorry to say I wondered so, that I had a good cry. I could see you all at home sitting round the fire, and plenty of singing & dancing and everything for your comfort and there was I bundled up in a couple of blankets in an old barn, and only too glad to have that to sleep in, but still better days in store.

We are still at the Base and do not know whats going to happen to us. I am sorry to say that our sergeant who returned himself to the company is fed up with Transport so I expect I shall be made full corporal very shortly.

Well Mum & Dad I think this is all the news for now, so I must now close. Wishing you all a Happy New Year. Trusting you are all in the best of health.

Your loving son
Reuben

P.S. Fags are short

Love & kisses to all at home.

————

Sorting mail.

14/1/16

Captain Alfred Bland served with the 22nd Battalion, Manchester Regiment, in France from November 1915 until his death on 1 July 1916 at the Battle of Somme. This letter is chosen from an outstanding collection of letters he wrote to his wife Violet.

My only and eternal blessedness,

I wonder whether you resent my cheerfulness ever! Do you, dear? Because you might, you know. I ought, by all the rules of love, to spend my days and nights in an eternity of sighs and sorrow for our enforced parting. And by all the rules of war, I ought to be enduring cold and hardship, hunger and fatique, bitterness of soul and dismay of heart. Alas! what shall I say in my defence? Because not even Merriman can depress me, and as for the C.O. I am simply impertinent to him, while the dull routine of being behind the line fills me with an inexhaustible supply of cheerful patience. What shall we say about it? Would it rejoice you if I confessed to being utterly miserable every now and then? If I told you how I loathed war and hated every minute that prolonged it? if I admitted that I yearn hourly for my return, my final return away from it all? if I said that I hated my brother officers and was sick of the sight of the Company? if I described the filthy squalor of the village streets, the sickening repetition of low clouds and sulky drizzle and heavy rain, and the dreary monotony of ration beef and ration bread. Would you be glad or sorry? Oh! I *know* how sympathetic and sad you would feel, and I *know* you would *not* be glad at all. Would you? And if you *were* glad, you would be all wrong; because, even if these things were true, it wouldn't bring us together again, it wouldn't make me love you more, it wouldn't sweeten those embraces we are deprived of for the moment, it wouldn't strengthen our divine oneness one scrap. Would it? No, my Darling, thank the heavens daily that in all circumstances you will be right in picturing your boy out here simply brimming over with gaiety irrepressible. I am becoming a byword. Cushion says 'I *like* you, Bill Bland.' Why? because I am always laughing at everybody and every-thing, greeting the seen and the unseen with a cheer. And it isn't a pose. It's the solemn truth. So let us go back again to those imaginary admissions above. I am *never* utterly miserable, not even when I yearn most for the touch of your lips and a sight of my boys. Why? because I am in France, where the war is, and I know I ought to be here. And I don't loathe war, I love 95% of it, and hate the thought of it being ended too soon. And I don't yearn hourly for my final return, although I am very pleasantly excited at the possibility of 9 days leave in March, which indeed we haven't earned by any means so far. And I don't loathe my brother officers but love them more than I had dreamed possible, and as for my Company, why, bless it! And the mud is such *friendly* mud, somehow, so yielding and considerate – and I don't have to clean my own boots. And I have lost the habit of regarding the weather, for if it rains, we get wet, and if it doesn't, we don't, and if the sun shines, how nice! And as for our food, well, I've given you an idea of *that* before, and I have nothing to add to the statements made in this House on November 30 and December 6 last or any other time. No, dear whether you like it or not, I *am* fundamentally happy and on the surface childishly gay. And there's an end on't.

Post just going. Good night, darling.

Ever your

Alfred

In April 1915 Joseph Quinn
enlisted in the 20th Battalion,
King's Liverpool Regiment, and
served as a lance-corporal on the
Western Front. He was killed in
action on 30 July 1916 at the
Battle of Guillemont during the
Somme offensive. This letter,
written to his sister, is from a
privately printed anthology that
the family published after
Corporal Quinn's death.

France, 21.3.1916

My Dear Alice,

I suppose you are already feeling nervous now that you realise I am in
France? But whisper it gently! The Kaiser would feel nervous too – if he
only knew. But why feel nervous? I am sure if you could only see us all
here you would rather envy us as we bivouac under the clear, sunny sky
of France. Well, there is a great glamour about going to the front and getting
nearer that strangely fascinating firing line. There is a certain romance
about it; a certain sense of elation as we march from the camp with swinging step, with the band playing merrily as we pass through the cheering
crowds. The sentiment, too, is real on these occasions, and the "good-byes"
are not mere conventionalities. Here, human nature shows both its grave
and gay sides. On one hand, one of the soldiers bandies jokes with the crowd
as he passes, whilst near by a mother clings to her son and a little girl
to her father. Will they be dubbed hysterical in these unemotional days?
But away we speed on our journey. By three a.m. we are all asleep in our
particular carriage, when our slumbers are disturbed by the sound of music.
A band somewhere is playing "Should auld acquaintance be Forgot," but
as we stare out into the blackness of the night we see nothing. There is
a strange stillness, however, in the carriage as we speed on our way, and
the sound of the music grows gradually fainter in the distance. The stillness
is at last broken by a remark of one of our party – "Why the blazes do
they play a thing like that when you are going away?" said he. Our train
journey ended, we make towards the troop-ship. But before boarding we
have about half-an-hour for breakfast at a certain "rest" camp – (the irony
of it).

At last on board, a blast of the whistle, and away we go. Soldiers representing every regiment in the British Army seen to be aboard this troop-ship.
We rub shoulders with Highland laddies and Yorkshire yokels. What a
variety of types! . . . . Hurrah!, France is sighted – and what think you
do we see as we set foot on French soil for the first time? – a great poster
of Charlie Chaplin! Such is Fame! Then away up a great hill to another
rest camp, which over-looks the town. Here we shall be till morning, when
we depart for the base. How interesting it all is as we look round the camp
at night! In the canteens here there is a curious medley of soldiers. One
meets with men of all types and regiments. Men who have been at the
front – wounded, perhaps – and now back again. Here we sleep in a great
hut, huddled together so closely that there is little room to stretch ourselves
without damaging our neighbour's face. We are up early next morning,
and prepare to entrain for the base. At last we are off in third-class continen-
tals – very third-class! But who cares a "continental" for that? For are
we not getting nearer the real thing? At last we have ceased to be "show
soldiers," and now we can rough it with good humour. So on we speed
to the base. As we enter the Base Depot we seem to immediately lose our
individuality (so to speak) as a draft. The place positively teems with military life, and it makes us feel as insignificant as, say, a person entering
a crowded theatre through a door which, though small is in a very exposed
position. A perfect maze of tents encircles us on all sides as we march
through (saluting sentries as we pass) to our own particular depot. Here

A muddy trench on the Somme in the winter of 1916–17.

we meet a few old friends who came out with the draft before us. How we welcome each other! Towards evening we wend our way to the Catholic Club, which is quite close to us. This is the most popular resort of the soldiers of all denominations. Here they come for refreshments and concerts. As I enter, it is thronged to the door. The brogue is strongly in evidence, and just behind me I hear someone say, "Shure, the Irish are expected to go over the top to-morrow." Then I realise that it is St. Patrick's Day in the morning! Well, good luck, to you my Irishmen! Wasn't it St. Patrick himself who banished the snakes from Ireland? Perhaps you will be instrumental in banishing the human variety from France and Belgium! Then a panel door at the end of the club slides back, and behold! an altar. Those who are not Catholic make their exit and short prayers are commenced. Then away to our tents again. Phew! Fourteen in one tent – yet we manage somehow, and sleep the sleep of the weary if not of the just. The next day away to the training ground, and how interesting the journey is. But at last we are finished for the day, and looking around us, on a beautifully clear evening, we feel that we would not have missed the experience for anything. Here, as I write, a French aeroplane sweeps gracefully like a huge bird over the peaceful valley which lies beneath us. How incongruous war seems now, and how difficult it is to realise that the greatest war in history is raging some miles further up the line. It is great to be here! Write soon; a letter out here is a godsend!

———

Captain John Staniforth served
with the 7th Battalion, Leinster
Regiment, 16th Irish Division, in
France and Belgium.

B.E.F. 10.5.1916

My dear ones,

Thank you for your letter of this morning. Hardly a week seems to pass
without a Zepp raid at Hinderwell now. I don't like it at all. I think I must
bring home a platoon and reinforce your defenders; how would that be?

I wish you would come out here just for a flying visit and see what things
are like. It's impossible to describe half the unforgettable things one sees.
You'd have a long, long journey in a crawling train up to railhead, and
you'd tumble out at midnight into something like a big goods-yard, with
crates and bales of every sort under a brilliant white light from the arc-
lamps. Very faint and far away you'd hear a dull, heavy thump; that's
the guns firing, ten or fifteen miles away. Then you'd climb on an old
Putney or Cricklewood bus, painted battleship grey, with all her windows
boarded up, and she'd go rocking away into the night along the country
roads, swinging on two wheels round corners and skidding past shell-holes,
with the guns in front getting louder every mile. Then you'd turn into one
of the French routes nationales; one of the straight paved avenues of poplar
trees that lead up to the crash and flame of war itself. Every minute the
traffic would get thicker: strings of motor convoys, rumbling transport
wagons, ambulances going up (empty) and down (not always), lorries, lim-
bers, staff cars, and everywhere the despatch rider snaking his motor-
bicycle in and out of everything; for this is one of the big highways to
the front.

Then the bus would come to a few blackened shells that were once a
village, and you would be told it was unsafe to drive any further, and you'd
have to get down and walk. Before very long you'd top a little rise, and
then stand and catch your breath with the whole Front spread out before
your feet. Imagine a vast semi-circle of lights: a cross between the lights
of the Embankment and the lights of the Fleet far out at sea; only instead
of fixed yellow lamps they are powerful white flares, sailing up every minute
burning for twenty or thirty seconds, and then fizzling out like a rocket
– each one visible at ten miles distant, and each lighting up every man,
tree and bush within half-a-mile. Besides these you will see a slim shaft
swinging round and round among the stars, hunting an invisible aeroplane; and every instant a ruddy glow flashes in the sky like the opening
of a furnace-door and there is a clap of thunder from the unseen "heavies."
The whole makes magnificent panorama on a clear night.

Then you'd step down into a trench, and that would be your last breath
of open country for sixteen days, if you were staying with us. The rest of
your time would be spent in a world of moles, burrowing always deeper
and deeper to get away from the high-explosives: an underground city with
avenues, lanes, streets, crescents, alleys and cross-roads, all named and
labelled and connected by telegraph and telephone. 'No. 3 Posen Alley'
was my last address, and you reach it via 'Piccadilly,' 'Victoria Station,'
and 'Sackville Street!' After you've wandered for perhaps two hours in the
maze you'll see a hole at your feet with a mass of wires of all sizes and
colours running along the ground and disappearing into it. Go down
twenty or thirty feet, down mud steps, and you come into a low, long cave,
lit by candles stuck in bottles and a swinging hurricane lamp. At a table

at one side are a row of men sitting at telephones and telegraph instruments. On the floor are sleeping bundles wrapped in blankets and greatcoats; and at the end, screened off by a waterproof sheet, is the linemen's room, piled with drums of cable, instruments, repair-outfits, crooksticks, and all manner of stores. All over the walls are stuck files of messages, circuit-diagrams, "flimsies", receipts, tables of delivery-services, duty rosters, and other details of office work.

Take the nearest instrument, which controls the four company lines: four spidery strands running out into the darkness to four little caves half a mile away at points in the front line, where a man sits day and night with the receivers clamped over his ears, listening for the little sounds out of space. Over the operator's head hangs a switchboard of plugs and holes and lettered brass bars, by which he controls the whole system throughout the battalion. As he sits there he has his finger on the pulse of its whole life, and a stream of flimsies comes out continuously under his hand: reports, requests for ammunition, stores and bombs, returns, rolls, news and all.

The other instruments are the longer-range circuits: to the watchful guns a mile in rear, to the Brigade Headquarters in their chateau, to the Division, the hospitals, the flank battalions, and the long trunk-calls to Army Headquarters and further.

Hanging on the wall is a curious little instrument, which is "all face",

A soldier of the 10th Battalion, Gordon Highlanders, in the trenches at Martinpuich, on the Somme, August 1916.

and a most scandalous gossip. It is simply a recorder – not a transmitter at all – and its business is to gather up all the news that is passing through and shout it out like a gramophone. It wakes to life quite suddenly and gibbers and sings away contentedly, though nobody pays any attention to it, and gives away the most precious secrets. Two company commanders arguing over a bottle of whiskey, No. 14 Platoon's complaint of short rations, an indignant battery commander on the track of his Forward Observing Officer, a Very High Personage being strafed by an Even Higher (this to the huge delight of the Signal Office) – there is nothing hid from it. Altogether a most human piece of mechanism.

If you are in at about seven o'clock in the evening, you will see all the lines grow silent one by one, and a certain hush of expectancy in the Office. Even "Whispering Willie" on the wall feels it, and stops humming and buzzing away to himself. We are waiting for the day's casualty return: the tale of wastage that is flashed through taking priority over all other messages, every twentyfour hours; on and on, gathered up and consolidated afresh at every office on the way, until it arrives in London in one long Roll of Honour and appears before you at breakfast next morning. But it was here in the Signal Office that we knew of it first.

The big switchboard wakes suddenly, gibbers a moment, and falls silent.

A ration party from the 6th Battalion, Queen's (Royal West Surrey) Regiment, carrying food containers to trenches near Arras, during the bitter spring of 1917.

The operator draws a pad of flimsies towards him with one hand, and settles down to write. As soon as the message is finished and acknowledged, another company takes up the tale and adds its own quota, and so on through the whole four; and each as it is finished is tossed over to the Signal Clerk, who registers it, puts the office stamp and time of delivery on it, and passes it out for delivery to the Adjutant's dug-out. Five minutes after the last one has gone, the runner returns with the consolidated return and hands it to the operator at the Brigade instrument, who flashes it through to his own headquarters. Then the Signal Office wakes to life again, and soon every instrument is in full swing again and the whole dug-out is filled with their humming, buzzing, singing and clicking, and the rustle of paper, and the snores of the sleepers.

And a very weary Signal Officer glances through the day's files and registers, all docketed and done up in bundles, wakes his Sergeant, finishes this letter, kicks off his boots, and rolls himself in an invaluable Jaeger flea-bag for four hours' oblivion.

Billy sends his love; he wrote to you yesterday. Meinself I am well also.

Goodnight.

———

George Noel Cracknell wrote home to give his account of the Battle of Jutland, 31 May/1 June, 1916. He was serving as an Assistant Paymaster, R.N., in the light cruiser HMS *Champion*, attached to the 13th Destroyer Flotilla.

4 June · H.M.S. Champion

My Dearest Mums,

Now that the papers have published it I can tell you all about the scrap. When I wrote you the other day I thought you would have already known about it, hence my telling you I was safe and well; but they didn't publish it until after we had returned. Well it was an exciting episode in one's life. I don't want to go through it every day in the week. We were with the battle cruisers and were the first to sight the enemy in their battle cruisers and battlefleet. They were engaged at once and shells soon started falling round us like hail our lot were taking on the whole German fleet and fought them for about three hours when the Grand Fleet arrived and put a different appearance on things. The Huns immediately altered course South and made for home and lager but they got a fine hammering from our battlefleet first for some time. I was on the deck most of the time and saw mostly all of it – it was providence which saved us from being blown out of the water – shells, 12 inch etc. fairly rained round us. Saw the Queen Mary – about 440 yards from us go up in a puff of smoke and flame afterwards there was nothing more see only 6 or 7 saved. It was all a magnificent sight. Especially after our battlefleet engaged them. But the night was very thrilling the sky was lit up with flame and intermittent actions were going on all round us. Saw two or three ships on fire and one hun dreadnought blown up by a torpedo. We had a narrow squeak, ran into some German big ship who turned their searchlights on us and blazed away but did not touch us, although bits of shell were picked up on deck next day. I was up all night – you can imagine I wasn't disposed to turning in. Next morning we had the devil's luck, a torpedo passed within a yard of the stern and another passed under us! We should now be little fishes if there wasn't some one keeping an eye on us. I hope he will continue to do so. There's no need to be depressed – the Huns got a good hammering and lost more than you yet realise – if we cop them a little further from Berlin next time they'll be lucky to get their lager again in this life. I wonder if any of Huths late employees were with the huns. I hope they got it in the neck if they were. We passed a german ship sinking – though most of the crew seemed to have gone down. Next day on our return we passed through masses of corpses. Reminded me of the "Aboukir"* days – rescued several lots on rafts and in small boats but they had been adrift for hours and many died from exposure. It was a horrible sight. Doesn't it seem funny that Tuesday afternoon I was playing golf and 24 hours afterwards wondering when my time was coming – its a funny world. I'm enclosing you a few snaps taken a few days before the battle – although you might think it to look at them, I'm not the C in C. I'm sending Dad some in my next, so you can keep these yourself. Well I wished you many happy returns today over a "Martini" – I'm afraid leave is now more distant than ever, but it will come some day. I could do with only a weekend. Saw my late ship during the battle and my late Captain was giving them it hot in a ship just ahead of us. Which must be nameless. All our losses have been officially stated, theirs haven't yet! so don't worry. Thanks for Collens and when you feel like making another cake there are plenty to do it justice. Much love. Wish you could come here for a few days —

Ever yr affec son,

N

16th Middlesex Regiment,
29th Division,
France.
June 28th, 1916.

Lieutenant Eric Rupert Heaton went to France in February 1916 to serve with the 16th Battalion, Middlesex Regiment. This farewell letter was written three days before he was mortally wounded in the attack on 1 July 1916 on the first day of the Battle of the Somme.

My darling Mother and Father,

I am writing this on the eve† of my first action. Tomorrow we go to the attack in the greatest battle the British Army has ever fought. I cannot quite express my feeling on this night and I cannot tell you if it is God's will that I shall come through but if I fall in battle then I have no regrets save for my loved ones I leave behind. It is a great cause and I came out willingly to serve my King and Country. My greatest concern is that I may have the courage and determination necessary to lead my platoon well.

No-one had such parents as you have been to me giving me such splendid opportunities and always thinking of my welfare at great self sacrifice to yourselves. My life has been full of faults, but I have tried at all times to live as a man and thus to follow the example of my father. This life abroad has taught me many things chiefly the fine character of the British race to put up with hardships with wonderful cheerfulness.

How I have learnt to love my men; my great aim has been to win their respect which I trust I have accomplished and hope that when the time comes I shall not fail them.

If I fall do not let things be black for you be cheerful and you will be living then always to my memory.

*Aboukir; British cruiser, sunk by a German submarine in September 1914, in which Cracknell was then serving.
†The Somme attack, originally scheduled for 29 June, was in fact postponed until 1 July.

I thank you for my brothers and sisters who have all been very much to me. Well I cannot write more now. You are all in my thoughts as I enter this first battle. May God go with me. With all my love to you all. Always.

Your loving son,

Eric

———————

Pte D. J. Sweeney
8081 D Coy
1st Lincoln Regt
B.E.F.

Private Daniel Sweeney's Battalion, the 1st Lincolns, also took part in the opening of the Somme offensive. He wrote to his fiancée, Ivy Williams to give his account of the few days preceding and following the battle.

My Dearest Ivy

I am still alive and kicking also I am as happy as anybody out here, but so hungry but that cannot be helped. Well darling I expect by now you know all about the great battle. I told you when I was at home it would only be a few weeks but I am glad to say that the date of the attack was kept a secret until the very last minute also there were very few men out here who knew at what time we were to charge the Germans, that being kept a secret has meant this success. I am sure. Well dearest I know that you would like to know all about this Great Battle and I will tell you what I know and saw of this murder. I think I am allowed to tell you but it will be a truer storey than what you have read in the papers at least I think so. (I have not seen any papers for two weeks now)

Well dear on the 20 of June my Regt. were ordered to proceed into the trenches for how long we did not know. Well everything went fairly well until midnight of the 24. I was one of a party of men who were to go out with an officer (who is dead now I believe) to go over to the German lines and try and find out how strong they were and if possible try and spring a suprise bomb attack on them, but just as we were going to start we received orders that the Great Bombardment was going to start that night so that was cancelled. Well our artillery and trench mortars started and so did Fritz's artillery he did get the wind up he sent all his shells into our trenches and at last he stopped but we still carried on up to 4 o ck. of the morning of the 25th June then our trench mortars stopped and the artillery fired a few shells every now and again. Well Fritz began to puzzle us as he only fired a very few rounds that day. Well I have nothing of interest to say of rest of the day but just as it was getting dark the R. Engineers came into our trenches and uncovered the gass cilinders which we had brought into the trench a few days before and they began to fix the pipes into them. At 11 ock that night our artillery started and so did our gas (we had our gas helmets on) then when the gas started and had gone as far as it is to go before we attack then our artillery stopped but as soon as we stopped old Fritz's artillery opened out THINKING that we were attacking but we were not, we were all under what cover we could get, of course we had a few wounded and killed but that could not be helped as he was sending some very big shells over. Well everything quietened down about 3.30 a.m. On the 26th the remainder of the day was not so noisy, that night we kept him awake but his artillery did not retalliate much. Well the morning of the 27th came and the boys of my regiment also myself were beginning to feel the strain as this was our 7th day in the trenches well there were no signs of us getting relieved so we had to stick it. That night 27th Lieut. Kirk, the best officer we had in this coy called for volunteers to go with him over to see Fritz and to see what damage our artillery had done. Well every man in the coy would follow this officer anywhere but he only took ten of us, they always expect us Regulars to go on these "trips" as we are experts or supposed to be experts at the game. Well we took 8 bombs each and got on top of our trenches in line and a pice of string running from the left hand man up to the right so as we would not get in front of each other, well we crawled up to what was once barbed wire but now it was only little bits (and well we knew it as our hands were torn to pices with it, but that was nothing. Well the officer pulled the string that was the order for us to lie still while he went forward, he came back and we crawled on a little further and at last got very near

The 4th Battalion, Worcestershire Regiment, strike cheery poses for an official photographer as they march to the trenches.

looking into his trenches we could not see much but I received an awful shock which nearly made me give the show away – I heard someone in the trench and I saw him put his hand on the top of the trench and then bang and a flash that nearly blinded me – this is what happened – the man was a German Officer and at night each side fire a sort of rocket up into the air out of a pistol and it bursts into flame and shows all the "no man's land" up. I did get a shock and I was shaking like a jelly but our officer then pulled the string 3 times and we stood up and threw 2 bombs each into the trench and ran back to our own trenches as quickly as we could. We all got back before the Germans recovered from the surprise except 5, I was one of them I tripped over something and fell into a big shell hole and stayed there until Fritz had finished his rapid fire. We had 2 wounded but not bad I crawled in an hour afterwards a bit shook up but quite happy. Well dear the morning of the 28th came and our artillery and trench mortars gave them socks all day but Old Fritz did not retalliate much at

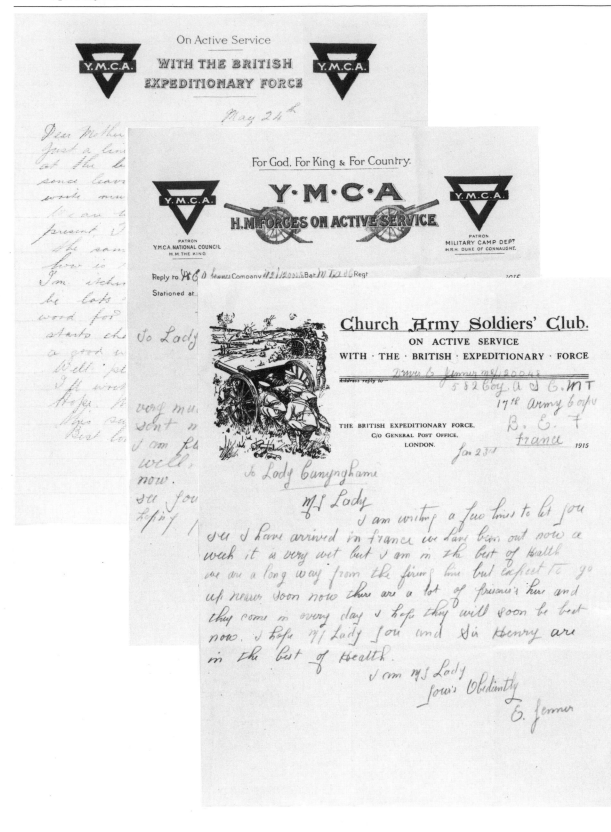

On Active Service
**WITH THE BRITISH
EXPEDITIONARY FORCE**
Y.M.C.A.

May 24th

For God. For King & For Country.
Y·M·C·A
H.M FORCES ON ACTIVE SERVICE
Y.M.C.A.   Y.M.C.A.
PATRON   PATRON
Y.M.C.A. NATIONAL COUNCIL   MILITARY CAMP DEPT
H.M. THE KING   H.R.H. DUKE OF CONNAUGHT.

Reply to

Stationed at

Church Army Soldiers' Club.
ON ACTIVE SERVICE
WITH · THE · BRITISH · EXPEDITIONARY · FORCE

Address reply to

THE BRITISH EXPEDITIONARY FORCE,
C/o GENERAL POST OFFICE,
LONDON.   *Jan 23rd*   1915

To Lady Cunynghame

My Lady

*I am writing a few lines to let you
see I have arrived in France we have been out now a
week it is very wet but I am in the best of Health
we are a long way from the firing line but expect to go
up nearer soon now there are a lot of prisoners here and
they come in every day I hope they will soon be beat
now. I hope My Lady you and Sir Henry are
in the best of Health.*

*I am My Lady
Your's Obediently
E. Jenner*

all we were greatly surprised. Well that night we gassed him again and he never fired hardly any shells back, and we never attacked but I bet poor Old Fritz was hanging in for us to do so. Well dear we were about done up as it was a terrible strain on anyones nerves, no sleep, and nothing else but shells day and night, but at last the order came that we were getting relieved. We were relieved at 3.30 a.m. on the morning of the 29th, and we were not sorry. The C.O.Y.L.I. that is the regiment that relieved us told us that they were making the charge but did not know when. Well we left the trench and went into some big dugouts about 2 miles behind the firing line and slept nearly all day on the 30th we cleaned up and had a wash and shave, the first wash for ten days, my word it was a treat "Sunlight" was "Bon" soap, some of the boys had scented soap but any old soap does out here we don't have time to study our complexion. Well dearest the 30th June was a very busy day for us we received orders that greatly surprised all of my Regt, and this is what it was, the attack was going to be made on the 1st July and we were in supports. On our way to the firing line every man had to carry something, some would get tools and water cans. I was rather unlucky I had to carry a box of 4 Stokes Shells which were no light weight. Well the morning of the 1st July came and I was very tired as we had not had much rest but it had to be done and no one knew even on the morning of the 1st what time the attack was being made but the artillery started at 6.30 and at 7.30 we heard the C.O. shout "The boys are going over" and where we was by getting on the hill near us we could see the boys going like mad across "no mans land" but we could not look for long as Fritz's artillery observers might have spotted us. At 8 o'c we began to move up and we had to go very slowly up the communication trenches as Fritz was shelling all of them, well we got our loads and after a very hot time we came into our own fire trench, now was the worst part of the job as we had to get up the ladders and get across to the German trench with our loads as quick as we could, how I managed it I shall never be able to say, but as soon as we were all on top the Germans started sending shrapnell shells – terrible things – well I heard when we got into the German 1st line of trenches that 15 of our boys were killed and wounded coming across, well we got into his first line and there we lost 24 men killed by 1 shell, buried them all I was blown against the back of the trench and just managed to get into a German dugout before 3 more big ones came. Well that night we had to go into the firing line and relieve the boys who had made the charge. We captured 4 lines of trenches that day not so bad. Well we got into them safe and we were there a few hours when he started his counter attack. We mowed them down in hundreds and never got within 20 yards of our trench he soon got fed up and did not try again that night. Well Dear we were in the fire line all night of the 1st also 2nd and we were relieved on the night of the 3rd by the 10th Division. Well we all came out by way of a road and we were lucky in not getting one man wounded. Well my Darling we are now out of hearing of the guns as we have had a 26 mile train ride, but when I dont think it will be long before we are into them again but at present we are not strong enough. I told you Dear that I was happy well so I am but I think of my poor dear old chums who have fallen I could cry. I have had to cry in the trench with one of my chums poor old Jack Nokes he has been out here since the very beginning of the war and has not received a scratch, he has never been home on leave because of a small crime, his home is at Wimbledon. Poor lad he died game with his mother's name his last word. I cryed like a child, not only him but a lot more of my poor comrades have gone. Ivy My Darling I am sure it is you and my poor sister praying for me that God has spared me. I said my prayers at least a 1,000 times a day (please God spare me to get out of this war safely for my dear Ivy's and my sister's sake). Ivy I cannot tell you the horrors of this war. You cannot realise what it is like to see poor lads lying about with such terrible wounds and we cannot help them. Well My Darling do not think that I am downhearted but it makes me sad when I think of these poor lads. Well My Dear I must finish this letter tomorrow as it is getting too dark now I know you will excuse the writing but I have only my knee and a little bit of wood to write on. We have come out of action with 4 officers out of 26 and 435 men out of 1150. I am glad to say that most of them are wounded, and I can say that for every 1 of our dead there are 10 German soldiers dead. I have accounted for 14 I am certain of but I believe I killed 12 in one dugout. I gave them 8 bombs one for Kitchner and the others for my chums. One German very nearly proved himself a better man than myself and he might have had me only for 2 of our men coming on the scene, we took him prisoner so he could not grumble, ("Mercy Cammerand") is all we could get out of him and "English very good". Well we took hundreds of prisoners that day and they were glad to be prisoners. but we made them work like slaves, we made

A trench in the Ovillers sector during the battle of the Somme, 1916.

them carry water and ammunition up to the firing line and some of them could not stand when we had finished with them. I have forgotten to tell you about the charge my regt made on the morning of the 3 July. There was only one piece of his last line of trenches which we wanted taken and the 1st Lincolns were picked to do it and we did it to we had to charge into a big wood and a wood is a terrible place to take. Well after ten minutes bombardment we went off towards their trench and we were met by a terrible machine gun fire which knocked a lot of our boys over as soon as they saw us coming they left their trench and ran into the wood then we had some terrible fighting with bombs and bayonets the Germans had a machine gun in this wood and we could see it and only 1 man with it but he was a brave man we could not get near him. As soon as some of the boys got to close he started throwing bombs but at last he was shot in the head but he must have killed a lot of our boys before he went under. Well when we got into their trenches and looked around we were surprised there was a big dugout with an electric dinamo in it just like an electric station all the dugouts had electric lights in them this turned out to be a general headquarters. We captured 2 Generals and 1100 men in this charge not so bad for the old Lincs was it. Our General did not know how to thank us he was pleased. Well dear we left the trenches that night and next day we were in the train all our divisions and now we are getting fitted out again but I dont think we will be in action again for a few weeks. This division is the same one that was anialated at Loos and now it has got its name back again 21 Division 62nd Brigade. Well Dearest that is all I can tell you this time. I am afraid that you will not be able to understand half of it as the writing is very bad but I know that My Dear little Ivy will excuse me. Well Dear Ivy I received your letter of the 26 June also your card of the 20, and they made me so happy. I am glad to hear that Frank is in a better place tell him I wish that I was with him. Well darling I think your photo is splendid and I shall value it more than any other photo I have got in my book. I do not know when I shall be able to have mine done but I will at the first opportunity. Yes dear tell Flo I should very much like to have one of her photos. I think her a very nice girl and I am sure it must be nice for you to have a friend like her to work with I wish Flo would change places with me but I believe she would if she could. Give her my very best wishes and I wish her the very best of health.

Well My Dearest I think I must close now as I shall be in parade very soon. I have not the time to answer all your letter so please excuse. Give my fondest love to mother and dad and my very best wishes to Olive and Charles and Frank also your next door neighbours. So sorry I have not time to write more but I know Dear that you will excuse this SHORT letter this time. I have heard from my French lady and she is very pleased to hear that I am (engaged). I have also received a letter from Elsie and her mother, they are old friends of mine. Well Dearest I will now close hoping to be able to write again soon. Cheerio My Dearest. I close with fondest love and thousand of kisses I remain.

xxxxxxxx   Your Loving
    xxx   Boy
    xxx   Jack

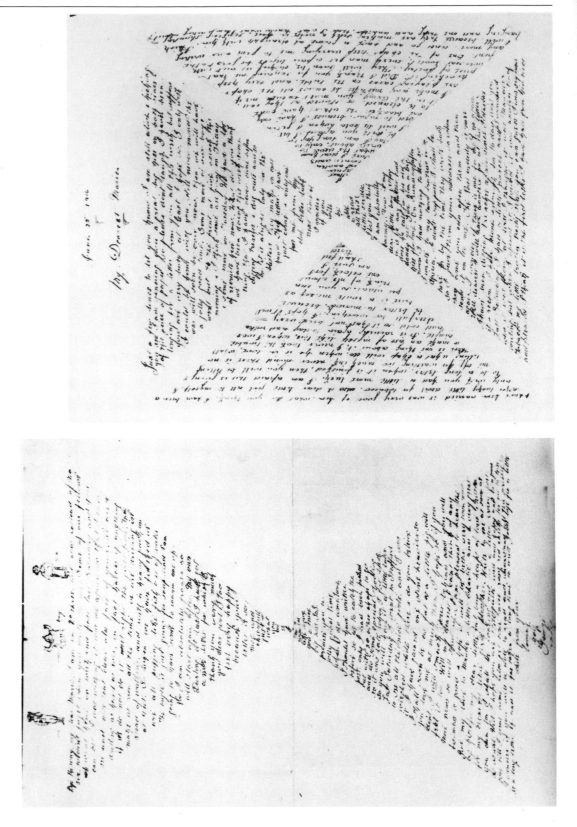

Percival Mundy enlisted in January 1915 in the Civil Service Rifles. He went to France at the end of June 1916 and was sent to the trenches almost at once. Private Mundy was killed in action on the Somme on 9 September 1916 while serving with the Kensingtons.

A letter to his wife from George Hayman, who served with the Lancashire Fusiliers. He wrote the text of his letter, on both sides of a single sheet, in the form of two large kisses.

July 7, 1916
Friday

Dear Father,

I guess you must be getting pretty anxious about me so I am seizing the first spare moment I have had since we left Havre. I managed to get hold of a field postcard yesterday and I hope by now you have received it, as even now I don't know whether I shall be able to get this letter through.

And now to give you the history of the last week. Before we left Havre we were told we were going to be attached to the Kensingtons instead of the C.S.R., much to our disappointment. It took us nearly a couple of days to complete our train journey and we stopped a little while at Rouen where I sent you a postcard. I'm glad to say that we didn't have cattle trucks. We de-trained about 12 miles behind the line, absolutely fagged out, for the little sleep we had had was of a very disturbed and uncomfortable character, as we had spent two nights in the train. We were told at this place that we should be there a day or two very probably. We had not seen a paper for some time so had no idea that the usual trench warfare was not still on. Judge of our emotions then when we were informed that the advance had begun and that after all we were to start off that same evening. We suddenly realised what we were in for! I shall never forget that Saturday night as long as I live. Imagine us, one hundred dog-tired men, starting off each with three quarters of a hundred-weight on his back, to march away to what we did.

It was a scorching hot evening and now and then a man would drop out, but at last with footsore feet and dirty perspiring faces we staggered into a village about 3 or 4 miles behind the line. It was crowded with soldiers who looked at our badge with curiosity. But their curiosity turned into amazement when one of our fellows started singing a Regimental March. In a moment it had rippled down the column and we marched into the market place singing "God Bless the Prince of Wales". I heard one soldier say to another: "These poor beggars can't know what they are in for".

We thought perhaps we should be billeted in the village for the evening but no such luck was ours. After a brief halt, we were served out with shrapnel helmets and off we went again.

It was now quite dark and the sound of the terrific British bombardment was indescribable. We suddenly emerged onto an open plain on the horizon of which was a sight which would have put a Brock's Benefit at the Crystal Palace to shame. I can't tell you what it was like. It's beyond me. The rumour was that we were going into some reserve trenches some way back from the front line, there to join our new battalion. This turned out to be right, and to cut a long story a bit shorter, we slept or tried to, underneath the stars. Early on Sunday morning we toddled off by platoons in order to avoid a rather cursory German shell fire and eventually we got back to the village we had entered and left the night before, and which I will call X. We rested in an orchard and in the evening we started off to occupy the front line trenches. We left them yesterday after a sojourn of 4 days and now I am billeted in a barn at X and have had some real sleep and also a wash and shave, luxuries denied to me for a week

In the trenches most of the work is done at night. If you are not a sentry you are on a working party or patrol. Of course, during the daytime a periscope is used but as twilight draws on the order "Stand to" is given and everyone hops up onto the fire step till it is quite dark and then gets down again leaving the sentries only on guard. The reverse happens at dawn.

My first day was fairly unexciting and gave us a chance to get fairly used to the noise but on Tuesday evening they began chucking over rifle grenades, which kept us on the qui vive. On that same evening we ran short of water and 3 from our platoon, Jim Stephenson, and a youngster named Barrett and myself went back to the village (which was being shelled like billio) in order to get some, and we were under shrapnel fire nearly all the way. But the worst of it was (and it struck me as being very ironic) there had been a big thunderstorm in the afternoon and the communication trench was ankle deep in water all the way and sometimes to the knee. You can guess I wasn't feeling very cheerful when I got back but when I was detailed to go up the same trench after dark to get some scoops, to say I was "fed-up" feebily describes my feelings. The following night I was on a party "bailing out"(?) the trench so I had wet feet for nearly forty eight hours.

Of course in civil life I should have caught pneumonia or rheumatic fever but you don't do that in the army. Fortunately, we have all had hot baths this morning and I am feeling quite cheerful about the feet once again. I don't know how long we shall "rest" here but it will be for a few days at any rate.... When you write next will you send me the number two Daily Mail War Map and also a newspaper or two as the only news of the advance that I have seen so far is a glimpse of one of last Sunday's papers I saw this morning. Anything to read is always welcome.

You might tell anybody who enquires about me that it is awfully difficult for me to write just now.

Hope you are not worrying about me. I am as right as rain. Love to Ruby and Miss Simms.

Your affectionate son, Percy.

———

This letter was written by Harry Waldo Yoxall, while serving as a lieutenant in the 18th Battalion, King's Royal Rifle Corps. Later he was awarded the Military Cross. Son of a Liberal M.P. he was to make a distinguished career in journalism.

23rd July 1916 [France]

Dearest Mother,

The twelfth Sunday! It seems an age, but great things have been doing in the meantime and the boys are much nearer home now than we thought three months could have brought them. There are high hopes everywhere now, not only among the trench men, who, having the best cause to be pessimistic, have always been the most optimistic, but also among the people who know. Of course it won't be easy, because the Bosch has still got plenty of fight left in him, but he can't stick the pace much longer.

It's the pace that kills, and if you set a killing pace you can't expect to come out unscathed yourself. Our losses are terrible, but probably it is more economic of life to spend it freely now and avoid a long-drawn war of attrition with its steady wastage. I know how terrible the cost must seem to all of you who are waiting at home, because each time I lose a friend all the joy of living seems to go for a moment, and it must be much worse to lose a father or son or brother, a husband or lover. John's loss is a very heavy one, and I have felt it more than any since Barnett went. He was straight and clean and simple and brave: a very fine type of public school-boy. Unfortunately it was not until my last year at [St.] Paul's, particularly after Robert left, that I got to know him, but in a short time we became very good friends and I am very sad now.

But it is not for John, though he has missed many happy years of life, as much as for his people. He did not die in battle but he died for England which is not a hard fate however early it comes. The only difficulty in facing death is the fore-knowledge of the grief of one's people. If we knew – and with many we do know: I know it of you all – that if the worst happens those at home could drown their sorrow in their pride, then it would be very easy. That is why death in war is so much easier than death in peace, where the consolation is so much less and we can only fall back on faith in a future life, which some have not. But in any case we think too much of the act of dying and too little of the state of death: and even the act of dying is generally swift and painless. Even Langford, who lingered for a day with twenty pieces of rifle grenade shrapnel in him, felt very little pain and to the last believed that he was getting better.

So if you at home can bear the cost we out here can endure the expenditure, even though it be of ourselves, very lightly. Remember that it is only by more sacrifices that we can save the sacrifices of the past two years from having been made in vain.

I was talking to Melvor, one of our trench mortar officers who is a very good friend of mine, on this subject last night: it arose out of the death

Two salvaged sewing machines put to use as a writing desk, Arras, 1917.

of Wingfield. He told me that he had watched our farewell from the ante-room window at Ranullies and he said that he had often thought of you all, and you, dear Mother, in particular, and admired your brave cheerfulness. You cannot think how the remembrance of it and the knowledge of its continuance helps me too. Of course I am in a very safe place now, but I hope one day to return to the line and take my part in battle. Thinking of that I do not feel that I shall fear anything: and fear is the most terrible enemy.

I'm afraid that this has been rather a solemn letter, but please do not jump to any dismal conclusions from it. These thoughts were simply prompted by the news of John's death and I wanted to say them to you so that you should know how I feel. I am well and busy, and happy in the feeling that the work we have put into this school is daily bearing better results. So now goodbye for the time.

With best love to you all,

Harry.

————

20th September 1916
France

Lieutenant The Honourable Edward Wyndham Tennant served with the 4th Battalion, Grenadier Guards, during the First World War. The author of the poem *Home Thoughts from Laventie*, he was known to his friends as Bim. He was wounded in action on 22 September 1916 during the Battle of the Somme and died two days later.

Dear Mother,

Tonight we go up to the last trenches we were in, and to-morrow or the next day we go over the top. Our Brigade has suffered less than either of the other two Brigades in Friday's biff on the 15th, so we shall be in the forefront of this battle. I am full of hope and trust, and I pray that I may be worthy of my fighting ancestors; the one I know best is Sir Henry Wyndham whose bust is in the hall at 44 Belgrave Square, and there is another picture of him on the stairs at 34 Queen Anne's Gate.

We shall probably attack over about 1200 yards, but we shall have such artillery support as will probably smash the line we are going for; and even if the artilllery doesn't come up to our hopes (which is very unlikely) the spirit of the Brigade of Guards will carry all resistance before it.

O darling Moth', the price of being in so great a regiment! the thought that all the old men "late Grenadier Guards" who sit in London clubs, are thinking and helping about what we are doing here now!

I have never been prouder of anything, except your love for me, than I am being a Grenadier. The line of Harry's rings through my mind: "High heart, high speech, high deeds, 'mid honouring eyes." I went to a service on the side of a hill this morning, and I took the Holy Communion afterwards, which always seems to help one along, doesn't it?

I slept like a top last night and dreamed that someone I knew very well, but I can't remember who it was, came and told me how much I had grown.

I feel rather like saying "if it be possible let this cup pass from me," but the triumphant finish, "nevertheless not what I will, but what Thou willest" steels my heart, and sends me into this battle with a heart of triple bronze.

I always carry 4 photies of you when I go into action, one in my note-case, two in that little leather book, and one around my neck. And I have kept my medal of the Blessed Virgin.

Brutus' farewell to Cassius sounds in my heart: "If not, farewell; and if we meet again, we shall smile."

Your love for me and my love for you have made my life one of the happiest that has ever been.

This is a great day for me.

God bless and give you Peace.

Now all my blessings go with you always, and with all my love.

Eternal love,
from BIM.

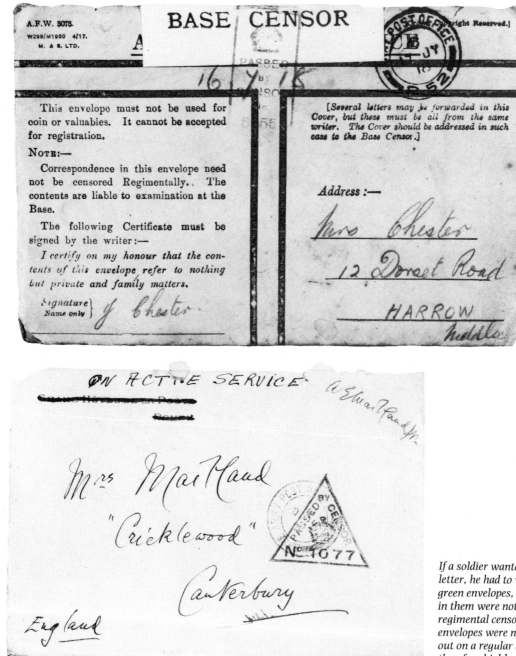

If a soldier wanted to write a private letter, he had to wait for an issue of green envelopes, as letters contained in them were not subject to regimental censorship. Green envelopes were not usually handed out on a regular basis and were therefore highly prized.

Private John Parker served with the 1st Battalion, Royal Fusiliers. He was killed in action on 31 July 1917, on the first day of the third Battle of Ypres.

France. [Undated]

Dear Harry,

In my last letter to Jess I promised to write you, so here goes. It is a rough night, raining, and the wind blowing at the rate of umpteen miles an hour. Thank goodness I am on gas guard for the next 24 hours (we are in the reserve line) 2 on and 4 off. The dug-out I am in is fairly comfortable and we have a decent fire in the brazier and I feel on good terms with myself for I have just heard that our fellows have taken Bapaume and that the French have progressed and that the cavalry are in action on the Somme. I hope that what I have just heard is true. Thanks very much, Old Man, for the two packages of "Clarions" you sent me. They have been very handy these last few days and I have enjoyed them immensely in spite of our heavies that have been going it some not very far behind us. Our division's artillery is reckoned to be of the best and when they strafe you bet old Fritz knows all about it. Our bread ration to-day has been a little short. We only had one loaf between eight of us. Of course, we had nearly a sand bag of biscuits to make up the deficiency. I have not long ago finished my tea and it took me nearly an hour to get a biscuit with butter and jam on it down me. I was finishing the last bite when I found that I was chewing one of my artificial teeth. That makes the third one I have had gone West. If I lose any more I am afraid I shall have to go in for an Army issue of upper ones. I hope they will fit better than the lower ones the Army gave me – I am wearing those in my pocket. Still, I shan't complain as we are here to kill Germans not to eat them. I find that the best way to get on with the biscuits is to grind them into a powder and make porridge of them. It really is a good porridge if cooked properly and sweetened with jam or treakle, and we have plenty of the two latter commodities in stock and also some raisins so you bet your humble is having a good supper tonight.

. . .

I am still in the pink and feeling fit though how we chaps manage to keep well in spite of the roughing it is beyond my understanding. It amuses me to think how I would change my boots at the least sign of dampness. Out here one can sleep quite comfortably in soaking wet clothes and get no sign of a cold. I really believe a kip in a good bed between warm blankets would make me ill. Well, Harry, I must draw to a close. You must excuse my writing on both sides of the paper. I do so because it makes the letter less bulky and at the same time it saves paper. Please give my fondest love to my dear Jess and the darling Children. I do hope they are in the best of health. Give my love too, to Sarah and Dad and the children and to Fan and her kiddies and accept same for yourself.

Your affectionate
brother Jack

———

4 February 1917

Calais

Eric Marchant joined the 7th Battalion, London Regiment as a private soldier in November 1914, and served with them in France in 1915 and again in 1916. He was later commissioned and once more left

Dearest Mother, I think my last letter brought me to Friday night so I will carry on with my recital from that point. Before I start however, I will just repeat what I said in my last letter in case it should not reach you.

for France on 29 January 1917 to join the 1st Battalion, Essex Regiment. Lieutenant Marchant was killed on the opening day of the Battle of Cambrai, 20 November 1917.

I am giving each of my letters a serial number, that is, all my letters addressed to Langham Road: this as you see is Number 4 and by this means you will know if you don't receive any of my letters. . . .

I am keeping a list of the numbers and will tick up each one as it is acknowledged. So far I have not heard from anybody, and reckon I ought to hear by tomorrow morning.

This sudden change in the ink is due to the fact that I have started using that tabloid ink for the first time. I think it is quite a success although I had to break through ice to get the water. . . .

This morning I spent the whole time censoring letters. This is the first time I have had this job and though it is rather irksome after an hour or two I found the letters of absorbing interest.

I suppose there is no better way of getting an idea of the spirit of the men and I won't deny that I was surprised at the tone of practically all the letters. The percentage that showed a realisation of religious truths and faith in God, was tremendously bigger than ever I suspected, and such phrases as "we must go on trusting in God" were in dozens of the letters I read. In particular I noticed one letter from a young fellow to his brother who was in the trenches and had evidently been out here some months and was getting badly "fed-up". The letter was worth printing if it had not been so sacred. The spelling was execrable and the writing almost illegible in parts but, strange to say, there was very little that could be called ungrammatical, and I am sure that the recipient will be cheered and helped beyond all measure when he gets it. In practically all the letters came the request "Write as often as you can" and nobody can doubt that the letters and parcels from "Blighty" keep up the spirits of the men as nothing else can.

You must remember that the men in this camp are of a very different class to the 7th London. There were not more than two or three letters in the whole bag addressed to London and the majority were going to little unheard of villages in Cambridgeshire and Suffolk. There was much to

A mule team and limber in difficulties, near Potijze Farm, in the Ypres Salient, October 1917.

laugh at in the quaint spelling. Quite a number always spelt 'here' as 'hear' and one man spelt 'used' as 'Youst'! All express their firm conviction that the war was 'nearly over' and one breezy optimist said that he thought 'pece terms was already ben (being) arranged and shud (should) wake up one morning and find ourselfs (ourselves) orf to Blighty agen'.

Altogether I found the duties of a Censor Officer most entertaining.

This afternoon it was too bitterly cold and slippery underfoot to go out so I stayed by the fire in the mess tent and read an extraordinary yarn by Max Pemberton called "Pro Patria" which I found more amusing than edifying. This evening I hope to go to a camp service if there is one. Everyone in the Mess seems to be contracting a "churchyarder cough" but so far I have kept clear of that and similar ills. The weather still continues extremely cold but dry and sunny, and I hope it will continue so, but the wind seems to be veering round to the west this afternoon so I suppose we must not be surprised if the rain comes into its own again, with its attending evils.

Well, I have no more news of interest at present so will close, give my love to all. Hoping to hear from someone shortly,

Your loving son, Eric.

Gunners of a Royal Horse Artillery battery writing letters near Hooge, September 1917.

Captain John Coull served with the 23rd Battalion, Royal Fusiliers. His farewell letter was eventually forwarded home after he was killed in France on 30 September 1918.

France
2.4.17   1 pm

My dear boy Fred,

This is a letter you will never see unless your daddy falls in the field. It is his farewell words to you in case anything happens. My boy I love you dearly and would have greatly liked to get leave for a few days to kiss you and shake hands again, after a few months separation, but as this seems at the present moment unlikely, I drop you this few lines to say "God bless you" and keep you in the true brave manly upright course which I would like to see you follow.

You will understand better as you get older that your daddy came out to France for your sakes and for our Empire's sake. If he died it was in a good cause and all I would ask of you dear boy, is that you will keep this note in memory of me, and throughout your life may all that is good attend you and influence you. May you be strong to withstand the temptations of life and when you come to the evening of your days may you be able to say with St Paul "I have fought the good fight".

Goodbye dear boy and if it is that we are not to meet again in this life, may it be certain that we shall meet in another life to come, which faith I trust you will hold on to and live up to.

I remain ever
Your loving Daddy
J.F. Coull

Corporal Ernest Foster's letter was written to the parents of his fallen friend, Frederick Fairhead, who had been a Bombardier in his battery in the 62nd Brigade, Royal Field Artillery. Fairhead had been killed four days earlier during operations on the Western Front.

45415 Corporal E.Foster
A/62 Bde. R.F.A.
12/6/17

Mr. and Mrs Fairhead,

Please allow me to express, on behalf of myself and chums, the deep and very real sympathy we feel for you in your bereavement. I want to write the kind of letter that is calculated to cheer you a little and if I am too clumsy please remember that is my intention and forgive me. First let me assure you that Fred's death was by no means a lingering painful one nor was he disfigured in any way. And secondly let me tell you that he died as I knew he would; like a real Englishman. He was struck in the chest and simply said "I'm done boys" and passed quietly away. We brought him down and at 6 pm on the 10th buried him decently in a little English cemetry close by here. Today some of the boys got away for a little while and brought back some nice little rose trees and other plants so tomorrow if his cross is finished we shall go up and do our little best for one whose cheerful presence is missed by a good many. Possibly you have heard of me through Fred. He and I chummed up about twelve months ago when he joined C. Battery and have been good friends in good times and in bad times ever since. Since the advance we have worked together most of the time and I think I may say, have had some tough jobs to handle but whatever the job or whatever the conditions Fred Fairhead was never a shirker nor was he ever anything but cheerful. I for one, shall miss him in a good

Making a cross to mark a soldier's grave.

many ways and having known him so well can understand fully what a big trial his loss will be to you. I am by no means a good Christian but last night I said just a little prayer which I shall repeat tonight. That you may be given strength to bear your affliction and every possible consolation. And now I will close hoping I have accomplished what I set out to do, and with my very best wishes to all of you believe me to be yours very sincerely.

Ernest Foster

P.S. When next you write to Frank will you please tell him I shall be pleased to see him or hear from him at any time.

———

B.E.F.
Sat 20th July 1917

James Milne was a company sergeant major with the 4th Battalion, Gordon Highlanders. On the eve of battle in July 1917 he wrote his farewell letter. In the event Sergeant Milne came through unscathed and survived the war.

My own Beloved Wife,

I do not know how to start this letter or not. The circumstances are different from any under which I ever wrote before. I am not to post it but will leave it in my pocket and if anything happens to me someone will perhaps post it. We are going over the top this forenoon and only God in Heaven knows who will come out of it alive. I am going into it now Dearest sure that I am in His hands and that whatever happens I look to Him, in this world and the world to come. If I am called my regret is that I leave you and my Bairns but I leave you all to His great mercy and goodness, knowing that he will look over you all and watch you. I trust in Him to bring me through but should He decree otherwise then though we do not know His reasons we know it must be best. I go to Him with your dear face the last vision on earth I shall see and your name upon my lips. You, the best of Women. You will look after my Darling Bairns for me and tell them how their Daddy died. Oh! how I love you all and as I sit here waiting I wonder what you are doing at home. I must not do that. It is hard enough sitting waiting. We may move at any minute. When this reaches you for me there will be no more war, only eternal peace and waiting for you. You must be brave my Darling for my sake for I leave you the bairns. It is a legacy of struggle for you but God will look after you and we shall meet again when there will be no more parting. I am to write no more Sweetheart. I know you will read my old letters and keep them for my sake and that you will love me or my memory till we meet again.

Kiss the Bairns for me once more. I dare not think of them, My Darlings.

Good Bye, you best of Women and best of Wives my beloved sweetheart.

May God in His Mercy look over you and bless you all till that day we shall meet again in His own Good time.

May He in that same Mercy preserve me today. GoodBye Meg

xxxx	Eternal love from
xxxx	Yours for Ever and Ever
	Jim

Somewhere,
23rd July 1917

Private Frank Orchard, who had joined the Royal Army Medical Corps because he felt such a strong hatred for war, was serving with the 1/5th London Field Ambulance in Belgium when he wrote this letter. He survived and became a Methodist Minister.

My dear Father,

It's some time since I wrote you, so I thought I would do so by way of a change. How are things conducting themselves round Heathfield, are people still as determined to exterminate every man jack of the enemy nations? Or are they getting a little common sense into their thick heads? I know if some of these so-called "patriots" were to come out here and see the horrible state they were creating out here by their tomfoolery they would (I hope) be very much shocked or stricken with remorse by the irretreivable damage they had caused, through their thoughtlessness. The people at home don't see the horrible sights that are to be seen out here, young men's bodies which were made to be of use to the Almighty one might say, to use a well used expression, temples of God, crushed and mangled, blown to pieces, by their brother man, with whom they have no real quarrel. But Father, I know the blame will not be laid upon the lads out here, because they think and believe they are doing the right thing, (I am speaking in the general sense) but the blame and punishment is *already* being borne by the demons who started the thing, and are prolonging it as long as they can, so that they may haul in more millions of money regardless of what it means to millions of men, women and children, who for want of a leader and organisation, are powerless in their relentless and cruel grip. How is the "P" movement progressing? Push it on as fast as possible, not only for our sakes, but for the women at home's sakes, and the women in all countries. I saw Will last night and had a glorious walk with him, we are both in the best of health.

Goodbye. My best love to Mother, and Toby and yourself.

From your loving son Frank.

November 11th, 1918

When he wrote this letter home from the Western Front, on the day the Armistice was signed, Lieutenant Colonel William Murray, who had been in France since 1914, was commanding the 15th Brigade, Royal Horse Artillery, attached to the 29th Division.

My dear Father,

I thank you very much for your letter. I am so glad to hear you are settling in and feeling well. I am sure you will gradually feel more peaceful in your new surroundings and when you have gathered all your belongings and books around you and found new friends you will feel you have found a haven of rest. We ceased fighting today and I have seen the last shot fired. A thing I never dreampt was possible in my wildest dreams. To have come through four years of this seething mass of horror and death is a truly wonderful thing and one for which no human thankfulness can be adequate. The last two days was very wonderful. We were pursuing a routed army. I and an infantry brigadier headed the advance and as the population saw us coming they went quite mad. They thronged round us and screamed and yelled like madmen. Old and young made wild attempts to embrace us they decorated our horses and guns with hundreds of flags till we looked like a travelling circus. Every church in the country was peeling its bells. As we reached the town the leading battalion which had got its band with it played the Marseillaise and the Belgian National Anthem. It was the most extraordinary scene of emotion. They all wept like children. Now we are sitting down wondering what we shall do next. Europe is in the melting pot. I pray God England won't follow suit. If we can only keep our heads and show we are a great nation at peace as well as war all will be well but I am a shade doubtful. Please thank Claudine

for the letter, I shall write soon. No more danger no more wars and no more mud and misery. Just ever lasting peace it is a great world. I hope I shall see you soon.

    Yours affectionately,

    Bill

————

On 24 November 1918, three days after the surrender of the German High Seas Fleet, Frederick Holman wrote home from the destroyer HMS *Versatile* to give his eyewitness impressions of the events of this historic day.

    HMS Versatile
    24.11.1918

My own dear Edie,

DORA* is now dead and letters will no longer be censored. cheers. loud and prolonged cheers. Well, in the first place I will tell you where we are or try to. We are miles from anywhere. Water! Water everywhere, we lost sight of land about 4 o'clock this afternoon. It is now getting on for 7 o'clock so we are about 60 miles from Scapa Flow. We are on our way back to the Firth of Forth having left Inchkeith yesterday morning with 20 German destroyers which we escorted safely to Scapa where they are interned. Well darling, as you have not had many letters lately I will try and give you a detailed account of what we have been doing, on that evening of Nov. 20th we found ourselves with other destroyers anchored almost under the shadow of Inchkeith Rock awaiting orders which we guessed would be to go out and bring the pick of the German Navy in. I turned in as usual and was called at 3.45 am as I had to go on watch at 4 o'clock, we had been under way about an hour and were just passing May Island. I was on watch in the Wheel House from which a good view can be obtained, and at about 7.45 we sighted them through the morning haze. Their Battle-ships, Battle Cruisers, Light Cruisers, and destroyers in one long line, stretching right out of sight, 74 ships, the pick of the German Navy. We were in four long lines, 125 destroyers, what we had behind the destroyers I do not know, the end being out of sight. We steamed to meet them and two of our lines went down one side of the Huns and two lines down the other side so our four lines were going in one direction and the Huns line down the middle of us in the opposite direction we steamed for three quarters of an hour at 12 knots, the Huns steaming at about the same speed. By this time the whole five lines were level. The signal was run up and as it was pulled down all the British Destroyers turned inwards in a half circle and now all five lines were going in the same direction, all in perfect order. It was a wonderful sight I can assure you. I don't suppose I shall see the like again, all this time all guns, torpedo tubes etc. were manned in case they should try their usual tricks, but nothing happened and we reached Inchkeith safely. In the afternoon our Captain, officers, and some of the crew went aboard one of the German boats to see if all shells, explosives etc had been removed, all of them were treated in this way and found correct. Our chaps said the place was dirty, the crews were dressed anyhow, the bread they saw was black, one man was having his

*DORA: Defence of the Realm Act

dinner which consisted of swedes and potatoes, the destroyers (ours) were complimented on the smartness in maneouvering and the way all our 125 destroyers dropped anchor the whole 125 anchors going splash together. The Commodore of the Flotilas being very pleased.

I always said they would never come out but when I saw that long line of armed might, the mighty ships of war of the second Naval Power in the world, I and every man aboard was amazed that such a powerful evil should have given in without striking a blow. I think all the world wondered.

If they had sent their whole fleet out the battle would have been awful. I don't think for one moment that they would have won, but they would have given us a terrible smashing and the loss of life would have been terrible, but they did not. Why! Goodness knows they must have had a horror of the British Navy, or else they must have had a fearful hammering at the Battle of Jutland, perhaps some day we shall know. For myself I am not sorry they saw fit to stay in harbour. Most of the German destroyers are now at Scapa. I was able to see the German crews quite near, they did not look starved, but nearly all of them were busy fishing to help the black bread down I suppose. . . .

Please keep this letter safe. I see the papers give a somewhat different account. They say we sighted the Germans at 9 o'clock for one thing which is quite wrong. They might have done so but we sighted them at 7.45. They were already sighted by scouts at 7.7. You can show this to anyone that you may think would like to read it but please keep it clean.

Love,
    FRED

THE SECOND WORLD WAR

Overseas

Here is the airgraph's destination,
nucleus of the guardian thoughts
from those at home who think of us.
This is the country which we might easily
have visited as tourists,
but with a camera rather than a pistol,
rubbing on the thigh.
Here is where we must forget
the numb bewilderment of separation,
and begin to learn
appreciation of new things,
such as the elegant ellipse
of Spitfire wings,
tilting and glinting in the sun.
Here the ties of tenderness
are stronger and delve back
into a precious past.
Here upon the battlefield,
the pawn on war's gigantic chessboard
can become a queen.
But with each coming night
a simpler thought prevails,
when soldiers make their bivouacs
into a fragile, private shell
tuned in across the waves
to England and their vivid home.

Alan White
Algeria

When England declared war on Germany in 1939 Edward Parry (later Admiral Sir Edward Parry) was commanding the cruiser HMS *Achilles* in New Zealand waters. This letter to his wife spans the days preceding and following the outbreak of war. He was still in command of the ship at the time of the Battle of the River Plate on 13 December 1939.

H.M.S. ACHILLES
Tuesday, 29th August 1939.

My little Sweetheart,

Although I hope this will never be posted, I must have a little talk to you before I go to bed. It does seem incredible (as you say in your little note, darling, which made me want to cry on my bridge today, when Kitney brought it up to me) that we are now on the brink of war again, and are being dragged apart by the actions of these madmen in Europe. Although I was half expecting it, I can't tell you how my heart sank when the signal arrived at 9 o'clock this morning telling us to go. It was quite silly of me really, for after all the other precautions which the Admiralty are taking, one could hardly expect them to leave a perfectly good cruiser sitting at Auckland doing nothing when the N.Z. Govt., had said she could be released. and as we left, Jim signalled that the "Leander" too is sailing tomorrow and that we shall probably get back first. I don't quite know what he means, but can only guess that —— and —— [*erased by censor*].

I just couldn't talk during our last few precious minutes together, darling – and didn't even say "Take care 'ooself, darling" as I meant to. I do hope you will go about and see people, and not let 'ooself get too depressed, darling. Why does great happiness always mean one has to be hurt so, sooner or later? If I didn't love 'oo so much, darling, today would have left me quite cold; and I might even be feeling that it was much better for us all, after our hurried preparations, to go to our war station and finish the job off. Whereas all I feel is one large ache, and a longing to turn the ship round and steam back to Auckland. When will that be, I wonder? How many of these beastly solitary nights have we to get through before we are together again? I think its the nights I funk most, particularly since I got into this habit of waking up in the small hours. By day one can distract one's thoughts more easily; but by night they take charge of one, and the only remedy is to switch on the light and read, which isn't a good one . . .

Thursday – or rather Meridian Thursday 31st (Friday in N.Z.) Well darling it doesn't look tonight as if there was a hope of avoiding War – This morning we had more encouraging reports, that Hitler had said he would negociate with the Poles, which he'd refused to do before. But I hear that on this evening's English broadcast he has more or less sent them an ultimatum – And about midday we got an order to prepare for war – though we haven't yet had the "warning telegram" which says that it's imminent. These last few days have been a succession of ups and downs – but I'm afraid there's no denying that the downs have been more prevalent. However we aren't at war yet – and I think we were just as gloomy last September – though as far as one can see there isn't much of a loophole left . . .

Isn't it awful to think that one man is responsible for millions and millions of people feeling just as you and I do.

Saturday

I suppose that this is our last night of so-called peace for many a long day – for I have little doubt that I shall be woken up some time tonight by

One of Bill Brandt's photographs of typical scenes in wartime Britain.

a signal saying we are at war again. I listen in to the Daventry broadcast, on Abbott's V.G. set, twice a day or so – as the ordinary Press telegrams are usually out of date – and it seems impossible to believe that somewhere in Europe open towns are being bombed – and that very soon England may be attacked from the air. I hope to Goodness they keep our twinks* away from London. However its no good worrying – and it is at least a great comfort to me, my little sweetheart, that you're well out of it. I think all we can hope for now is that Hitler's regime will crack under the strain of war – and be replaced by something a bit more reasonable. He must be afraid of his own people to have threatened them with heavy penalties if they listen in to foreign broadcasts . . .

Sunday

So its come! and I was woken up last night to be told we are at war again – and I did turn over and go to sleep again, without a very long delay! Its funny how one's ideas do re-adjust themselves to most things, isn't it? and its very merciful really. For if one allows one's imagination to think of what is going on in the world, and the awful things that will happen in the coming weeks and months, not to say years, one will go dotty.

Anyhow nothing can rob us of a jolly good 17 years, can it, darling? and I only grudge the times when we've been separated. And considering what my trade is, we've really had remarkably little even of that. I suppose its been too good to last, and that we must pay for having such happiness, before we become entitled to more.

Tuesday, 5th Sep

I simply can't believe that its only a week since we said goodbye, my little sweetheart – Actually its 8 days because of the extra one; but it seems centuries. And the prospects of mails are so poor that they are not worth thinking about at all. I'm afraid it will be longer than we expected before even this can reach you . . .

I should be quite content even now, with the whole world going mad, if you were here, although of course common sense must step in and say "No, You'ld be desperately worried really and you ought to be jolly glad that she's in such a safe place as N.Z."

But I mustn't pose as being too desperately mouldy darling. With such a jolly good crowd of officers, and, as you saw, a very cheerful ships company, I certainly would be a very miserable sort of creature if I allowed myself to get depressed. And so, darling, don't worry about me from that point of view, because I have plenty to occupy me. And I get taken right out of myself by reading, as you know; and I'm thoroughly enjoying re-reading my Stevenson's "The Black Arrow", "The Master of Balantrae" and "Virginibus Puerifsque" have followed one another in rapid succession. But so far I've enjoyed "Catriona" most; for it made me weep heartily, darling, and suited my silly sentimentality!

Friday 8th

Another three days gone . . .

We are still getting plenty of wireless news. It does seem astonishing

*Twins

that the Germans haven't bombed England yet. And that our propaganda-distributing machines have not yet been attacked. Whether it means that Hitler intends to go slow with us, or is only biding his time, or is afraid of offending world opinion, defeats us altogether. As he is using his submarines ruthlessly, one would have expected him to do the same with his aircraft. One longs to know more of what's going on . . .

Sunday 10th September
I'm due up on the Bridge now, sweetheart, for my last visit before turning in. Night! night! my little booful. How I wish I could do something to end this nightmare, which has hardly begun yet!

All my love is yours, sweetheart – and I only live for the day when we come together again.

Your own
 Ted

I have written to Lloyds Bank, telling them to let you overdraw up to £50 a month on my account when the blank cheques are used up.

––––––––

Sapper Jack Toomey had served with the 42nd Divisional Postal Unit in France in May 1940. This letter was written to his cousins two weeks after his return to England during the evacuation from Dunkirk.

42nd Div. Postal Unit.
Darlington.
Saturday.
[June 1940]

Dear Folks,
Just a line to let you know that I am still knocking about, had a letter from Mum this morning and was glad to hear that Aunt Edie was a lot better.

Things up here aren't too bad, we are billeted in a British Legion Club – beer downstairs blankets upstairs. An air raid warning twice nightly but such things don't bother us veterans who have been bombed from dawn to dusk nearly every day for three weeks, well, not much anyway.

Would you like to hear all about the War straight from the horses mouth. You wouldn't, good 'cos you are going to.

Before the war started we were enjoying a pleasant tour of France. Landed at Cherbourg, went south to Laval, in Mayeuse, had one or two trips into Le Mans with mails. From there we went N.E. to Evreux, stayed the night then onto Amiens here we stayed a week or so and moved on to the Belgium border at a place called Vervique-Sud on the Lys, to the south-east of Lille, and about ten klms south of Armentiers, we were staying here when the war started, after that we moved so fast and often that I didn't have time to take any notice of names.

Well, it started and after two days and nights of constant "alert" and all clears, we drunk a bottle of rum and another of Cognac biscuit to get some sleep, the air raid siren was in a church tower opposite and about twenty feet from our window. We were determined to sleep somehow. I was still drunk when I woke next day. A day or so later we were in a chateau farmhouse affair when a dog fight developed about a thousand feet above us Messerschmidts, Hurricanes and Spitfires were having a hell

of a good time. I don't know who won, I was too busy dodging planes, bullets, and AA. shrapnel. From that day onwards my tin hat stayed on my head – even in bed sometimes. Another day a twin Messerschmidt came into to M.G. an AA post near us only they got him first he hit the dirt at about 300 mph – very little was left of the plane, the pilot and observer was buried by the road with a prop: blade stuck over them. At another place they flew up and down the street, machine gunning as they went, nice quiet clean fun. At another place, the last before we made the Dunkirk dash, the dive bombers came over and bombed us in the afternoon. Never look a divebomber in the face, Bill, cos if you do you can bet your sweet life things are going to hum soon, but pray and pray hard and run, run like hell for the nearest ditches and dive into them. I got quite used to diving in the end, could make a flat dive from the middle of the road or a power dive from a lorry in one motion. Well, after the bombers had gone and we took stock of the wreckage and found we were all alive, they came back and threw out leaflets for our use.

Then came the order to move and a rumour had it that we were making for Dunkirk. Off we went, about half-a-mile in front of Jerry, after an hour we stopped and everyone went into the ditch, that is, except another bloke and myself who were jammed in the back of the lorry. We could hear M.G. fire and thought it was a quiet shoot up by Jerry planes but when tracer shells started coming through the roof of our lorry, I knew I was wrong. Two shells took a knapsack from the box next to my head and threw it out of the back looking like cotton waste another went past my ear so close that I felt the wind of it. All the time M.G. bullets were smacking and rickshetting off the struts. I just sat and gave up all hope of coming out of that lorry alive. However I heard a noise of a tank chugging past the lorry and the shooting stopped for us. The bloke driving the tank saw us in the lorry and calmly tossed a hand grenade under the tailboard! After it had gone off and we found we were still alive we came out of that lorry with our hands in the clouds. There are pleasanter ways of committing suicide than fighting five tanks, an armoured wireless car and a plane, with a rifle. Well, they took us prisoners and while we were looking after the wounded the French opened fire and we were between the two fires, so back into the ditch we went. The main body of prisoners were run off to a nearby village. We lay in the ditch in a thunderstorm for two hours and then went back to our own lines. So much for my "escape", more of a case of getting left behind. The engine of our wagon was so shot up that it fell out when we pressed the self starter. We managed to get a tow from our Ordnance and after ten hours we slung it into the ditch. We had got separated from our crowd and were alone in the middle of the night in France or was it Belgium, anyway we were lost, so we just ambled on until something came along – it did – one of our artillery crowds so we joined the arty for a spell. Then as dawn came up we found the main Dunkirk road and what a jam, after about ten hours of stopping and starting driving into ditches and back into lorries we got near Dunkirk, and here we had to dash thru' a barrage of shrapnel so we slammed the old bus into top and went flat-out down the road. When all was clear and we were on the outskirts of Dunkirk we stopped on a long raised road with the canal on either side and nice big trees sheltering us from the air. We got out

British troops being evacuated from the Dunkirk beaches, May 1940, and looked up – there were about seventy bombers (German make, naturally, we hadn't seen one of our planes for three weeks!!!) knocking hell out of the docks or what was left of them. From there to the beaches and they were black with troops waiting to go aboard only there were no boats. They gave us a raid that afternoon and evening and the following day they gave us a raid that lasted from dawn till dusk, about 17 hours. The fellows laid down on open beaches with the bombs falling alongside us lucky it was sand, it killed the effect of the bombs. At the end of the day there were about 8 fellows killed and injured out of about 100,000.

The following day dawn broke and we saw the most welcome sight of all about a dozen destroyers off the beaches and more coming up – boats of all shapes and sizes, barges, Skylarks, lifeboats and yachts. Fortunately the day was cloudy and misty, the bombers only came once and as they came low beneath the clouds the Navy let 'em have it. They slung up everything the guns, I never saw this action, I was scrounging for a drink, we hadn't had water for a fortnight it was too risky to drink and all we could get was champagne and wines. Spirits only made me thirstier. However on this morning I had a drink of vin blanc and had to sit down I was drunk as a lord, the last time I had anything to eat was about three days off, and on an empty stomach the wine had a devastating effect. That evening we went aboard after make dash after dash up the jetty to dodge shrapnel – Jerry had got close enough for his light artillery to shell us.

We got aboard and started, there were about 800 of us on one small destroyer. The Navy rallied round and dished out cocoa, tins of bully, and loaves of new bread. This was the first grub some of us had for nearly four days and the first bread we had for a fortnight.

When we were about an hours run off Dover and thought we were safe a bomber came down and slammed three bombs at us – missed us by six feet and put all the lights out downstairs. We got to Dover at 2 am and climbed aboard a train, we were still scared to light cigarettes, a light on the beaches meant a hail of bombs, and we just drowsed, at Reading we got out and shambled to the road outside it was about 8 am and people just going to work stopped and stared, we must have look a mob, none of us shaved or wash for a week, our uniform was ripped and torn, with blood and oil stains. I had no equipment bar a tin hat and gas mask, a revolver I picked up from somewhere stuck out of my map pocket. One or two old dears took one look at us and burst into tears. I dont blame them, I frightened myself when I looked into a mirror.

They had buses to run us to the barracks, we could just about shuffle to them, we were so done up. At the barracks breakfast was waiting and they apologised because it was tinned salmon and mashed potatoes, we, who had been on half or no rations for nearly three weeks were too busy eating. After grub we slept for a few hours and had dinner, got paid and changed our money to English, changed our uniform for a clean lot, had a shave, shampoo, haircut, and bath and breezed out for a drink of beer. We stayed here for a week and went to Bournemouth to be re-equipped. At Bournemouth, three Spitfires roared overhead one day just above the pier and over the beach. I was on the beach, laying flat on my face before you could say "Scarp". I just couldn't help it. Leaves a self preservation instinct or something.

From there we were sent up to here nothing much has happened, we work in the P.O. doing much the same as we do in civilian life. They, the army, did try to get us out of it into the country under canvas but we told them we couldn't work without a post office near us so they let us stay.

Thus ends my little bit of the epic of the battle of Northern France and Dunkirk.

The times were rather tough and altho' I was scared stiff for three weeks it was something I wouldn't want to have missed. My only regret was that one of our Rover Scouts was left behind.

Still, c'est la guerre.

> Chin, chin,
>> Love to all,
>>> Jack.

———

In the summer of 1940 Group Captain John McComb, R.A.F., then a squadron leader, commanded No. 611 (West Lancashire) Squadron, Fighter Command R.A.F., which saw service during the Dunkirk evacuation and the Battle of Britain.

Digby
3/6/40

My dear Mum,

Can't remember when I last wrote. I think about a week ago. Sonia is still away . . .

I've been all over the place the last few weeks. Slept in the Mess three nights. In a wooden hut once and a tent three times. We had another do over Dunkerque yesterday. We got 8 and lost Donald Little and Ralph Crompton. These two chaps shared the cottage next to us at the Annexe Wellington. Hard on the two wives but they *may* turn up. It's amazing the way chaps have been getting away with it and turning up days later. Jack Leather saw what he thought was Donald shot down by a Messerschmidt so Jack shot it down in flames and damn near in turn got shot down himself. Ken had half his aeroplane – all the hood and a damn great hole behind his head – shot by a shell. His controls were hanging by threads. He staggered home. Barry Heath got a bomber and other fellows got bombers and fighters. We were looking after another Squadron who were pasting the bombers.

I reckon we had 60 fighters to deal with. I had a scrap with two fighters. Got one and was so pleased with myself I forgot to shoot the other. Could have got him. I then gave two more the slip that got on my tail firing cannon shells, and got stuck into five Heinkel Bombers. I was by myself and thought it a trap but there seemed nothing behind or above so had a crack at them. I hadn't been there a second before a Messerschmidt 110 on my tail starting pumping shells at me. I did a roll out of that – getting too hot and in an effort to nip round on its tail I spun down 10,000 ft. to 2,000 ft. I went up again to 5,000 ft. and saw that there were only 4 Heinkels left so I *may* have got it, but the A.A. fire was so heavy that I don't think I could have made it again without getting hit, so I beat it home. Hell of a fight.

A.O.C. came down this morning and congratulated us. I think Crompton had his tail shot off. I saw a Spitfire spinning down, which might have been him, without a tail but there were so many aeroplanes that it was hard to make much out – there were so many of the devils one nearly always had to deal with two or three at once.

The other Squadron got 16 or 17 Bombers for certain, so we did our job O.K. Christ I was frightened at times, some of our machines looked like sieves. We'll get another bang at the bastards soon I hope, but for the moment we are licking our sores. I had mirrors fitted on all our machines, which saved a few chaps. Young Macfie, aged 19, chased one straight into the harbour and when the bits came up gave it a burst too. Brown (20) escaped by flying down a street in Dunkerque with a Messerschmidt on his tail and shook it off by diving under a crane!! His comments in his battle report was "Bet my performance didn't help the morale of the B.E.F. a hell of a lot". It's damned frightening but hellish good fun (afterwards). I got 70 minutes sleep in the 24 hours Sat/Sun. Bit tired last night.

I 'phoned Sonia last night who told me she had been speaking to you. Must write to Cty Offices – havn't written for weeks.

No time for more,

Love to both,
Jim

Sergts. Mess R.A.F.
41 Squadron,
Hornchurch.
Sat. [1940]

Dear Mother,

Herewith a line to let you know that I reached my base alright yesterday, & also an adventure to thrill the youth of the next generation & this one too I should imagine.

After lunch we went off on a "flap" & were patrolling London to Maidstone when we get the "tally-ho" & there is the old 109 stooge trap all laid open to the boys of 41 Sqdn, being clear we could see gangs right, left, up & down so off we go into line astern & climb into the sun so that the swine can't get such a big dive on us. Next minute something hit me amidships & most everything goes quiet after a few seconds of bumps, swings & jars & there I am sitting in the cock-pit of my Spitty with no engine & the tail & about a yard of fusalage hanging on by the *tail control wires*, & altimeter reading 28,000 ft. I sat still as I knew I wouldn't catch fire & I saw the other Spit tearing towards the deck, smoking slightly. Next moment however there is a bang & the tail comes over & bangs the cockpit by my ear, & swings back & takes another crack. So I lowered the seat & sat with all my straps undone. & wireless disconnected breathing in the oxygen which luckily is still coming through, & watching the tail having a crack at me. At 17,000 I decide to get out & grabbing the tail on one of its frequent swings, held on until I am standing on the edge of the cockpit & then let go & jumped backwards. At this time the wreck is going slowly round & the starboard main planes plonks itself under my back, & there I lay for about ten seconds wondering what I had landed on & looking around decide to get clear by going to the wing tip & stepping off by the trailing edge. I could now hear the battle above & so decided to do a delayed

Leslie Carter joined the Royal Air Force Volunteer Reserve in 1939. At the time he was eighteen and his father gave written consent so that he could learn to fly. Shortly after war was declared he was flying as a flight sergeant on missions across the Channel. He became a Spitfire pilot with No. 74 Squadron, Fighter Command, R.A.F. On 6 July 1941 he was lost on a sweep over France.

drop. I couldn't get my head up for a start until I decided to do what I had heard previously, double up my legs, & it worked, I started rolling. I whizzed down to lower cloud level at 4,000 feet & looked for the ripcord & pulled it, according to regulations. For less time than it takes to write a couple of letters I thought I was being strangled, there being no jolt, & then was leisurely floating down to South Kingsdown, ten miles from Maidstone, into the arms of about ten L.D.V.'S & forty women & kids demanding to know if I was British. I only had one minutes anxiety & that was when my wreckage came past, after I had pulled the rip cord, about fifty feet away. I have not a single cut or bruise thank the Lord & the parachute packer, whom I have just been round to thank in the normal way.

Cheerio, Love to All at Home,

Keep smiling, Les. P.T.O.

P.S. I must get the adjutant to send off for my *caterpillar*, as it was an Irving air chute.

———

12th August 1941

Robert Rafferty was born two days after news arrived that his father, Lance Sergeant Eric Rafferty had been captured two months earlier at St. Valery, France, on 12 June 1940. Sergeant Rafferty who was with the 51st Anti-Tank Regiment, Royal Artillery, 51st Highland Division, remained a prisoner of war in Germany for five years. Each year he sent his son a special birthday letter. This letter was displayed during the war at several P.O.W. exhibitions sponsored by the British Red Cross Society.

My Dear Son,

I have been here celebrating your Birthday to-day. One year old, my lad, and I have never seen you. Of course, your Mum has been sending me photos regularly and I know just how you look, and your Mum says you are a splendid little fellow, being so young Robert, has been a blessing to you my lad, what I would give to be in your shoes to-day, maybe you will better understand as you grow older and wiser, well there are 28 fellow comrades here and they are joining me in wishing you very many Happy returns of the day, we have had a great feed to-night Robert, your Mum will tell you when you are old enough to ask, I cannot send you any presents from this country, Germany, but I have bought you a few small items for your birthday son. Next year you shall have them. I know your precious Mother will have been very busy, shopping and all good friends will have laden your cot with a bountiful supply of presents, not forgetting your godmother, Aunt Gladys and Uncle Bob and the many good aunts and uncles who have taken a great and loving interest in you. I owe them a great debt Robert, the days of your life when I should most love to be with you, are alas for me, spent in confinement, however I am well and fit and know your dear Mum is looking well after you, Cheerio my Stout fellow, keep smiling and cheery, always be brave and honest, fear no Man and Life will be sweet to you. All my love sonny boy, my thoughts at night are always for and of you and Mum.

Thanks a million Mum.

xxx

Your Loving Daddy

Toodle oo the Noo

xxxxx   xx

xxx

———

Facsimile of Eric Rafferty's letter to his son, Robert, seen here in his mother's arms.

12th August, 1941.

Auf diese Seite schreibt nur der Kriegsgefangene!
Cette page est réservée au prisonnier de guerre!

My dear son, I have been celebrating your Birthday to-day. 1 year old my lad, & I have never seen you, of course your Mam has been sending me photos regularly & I know just how you look, & your Mam says you have been a jolly fine little fellow, being so young Robert, has been **a blessing to me** . . . what I would give to be . . . . you will better understand . . . . men, well there are 28 fellow . . . . They all join me in wishing you very many happy returns of the day, we have had a great feed to-night Robert, your Mum will tell you when you are old enough to ask, I cannot send you any presents from this country, Germany, but I have bought you a few small items for your Birthday son, next year you shall have them, I know your precious Mother will have been very busy, shopping, & all good friends will have laden your cot with a bountiful supply of presents, not forgetting your godmother, Aunt Gladys & Uncle Bob, & the many good aunts & uncles who have taken a great & loving interest in you, I owe them a great debt Robert, the days of your life when I should most love to be with you, are, alas for me, spent in confinement, however I am well & fit, & know your dear Mum is looking well after you, Cheerio my Stout fellow, keep smiling & cheery, always be brave & honest, & as an honest man a life will be sweet to you, all my love sonny boy, my thoughts at night are always on & of you & Mum, your loving Daddy. Thanks a Million Mum.
x x x

Toodle oo the noo
- - - - -

John Wyatt joined the East Surrey Regiment in June 1940. After six months of training he was posted to their 2nd Battalion, stationed in Alor Star, Northern Malaya. Because his unit was so badly depleted in the weeks following the Japanese invasion on 8 December 1941, it was amalgamated with the 1st Battalion, Leicestershire Regiment, to form the British Battalion. Corporal Wyatt's letter is an account of the Battalion's operations at Gurun on 14/15 December 1941. After the fall of Singapore, Wyatt became a prisoner of war in Japanese hands until 1945.

L/Cpl J. Wyatt
D Coy
British Battalion
Malaya

Dec. 21, 1941

Dear Mum and Dad,

Hope this finds you as safe and as well as I am at present. Before I start you will notice that my address is completely changed also that I think it best that you should all send me an occasional letter as all your letters have not reached me now for over a month and as things are they will take a long time to reach me so now and again to let me know how you all are. Well mum before I start I would like you to give thanks to God at Church for the mercy he has shown, not only to me but to the whole Battalion, 3 times. I have just waited for death but with Gods help I am still here, I have felt all along that with all your prayers God would keep me safe. I will only give you one instance of it 10 of us were in a trench in a little native village in the Jungle, we were told last man last round, for we were surrounded by Japanese and they were closing in on all sides. Some of the chaps were saying good-bye to each other and I was really frightened at the thought of dying but as the minutes dragged on I resigned myself to it, then all of a sudden 3 aircraft came over, was they ours? Was they be buggered, down came the bombs all round us. All we could do as we crouched there was to wait for one to hit us but that good old trench saved our lives for it swayed and rocked with the impact, about one minute after they flew off believe it or not 4 tanks rumbled up the road, and gave our positions hell they flung everything at us; grenades, machine guns, but still we crouched in that little trench, we could not return fire for if we showed our heads over the trench the advancing Japs were machine gunning us. All of a sudden we heard a shout, run for it lads, and we run, but that was the last I saw of the Brave officer who said it. I shall never forget him, as we ran past him, pistol in hand holding them off while we got away. I haven't seen him since. Anyway, we waded through about a mile of padi, reached the jungle in safety, then on to find the British lines. We tramped 20 miles that day living on Jungle fruits. The fight started at 7 in the morning, we reached safety at 5 at night. Then for sleep, food, clean clothes, shave, for we had been at the front for 8 days without sleep or clean clothes for we have lost everything, but thank God I am still here, most of the Battalion reached safety but a lot of poor chaps are still missing some of my friends too. We are all together now at a big Catholic school, the Brothers here are very kind to us. Excuse pencil as this is the first chance I have had to write in a fortnight, so please make do with this. Keep smiling and I hope to see you next year. XXXXXXXX Well mum, our worries are over. We have just been told that we are moving back, and our job is to stop looting and all our fighting is finished, am I glad. We certainly knocked the Japs about while we were there didn't we, we are miles better than them and we are sorry we won't be able to get another smack at them. I shall have to hurry as the candle is burning out. So I will say good-bye for now. Dorrie xxx Jimmie, George, Mrs. Ward Church, rest of family and neighbours. So please don't worry, God bless you all and keep safe. Your ever loving son JOHN V xxxxxxxxxxx

P.S. I shall have a lot to tell you when I get home. As usual Jerry is here with the Japs, German pilots and German N.C.O.s. Tell Dorrie that the corporal who wrote to her is missing but safe I think, and my sergeant who wrote to her got shot in the leg and is a prisoner I believe.

————

The following letter was written by Lieutenant George Morrison, who served with the 7th Battalion, Black Watch, in the Eighth Army. He was killed on the first night of the Battle of El Alamein, 23–24 October 1942.

19th September 1942

Dearest M——

I'm writing this one marathon seven day letter to make up for all the long ones I haven't or ever will be able to send you. As you know fine, this life is one of constant movement and change, and it is impossible to say when I'm going to be in one place more than a couple of days or so. But I feel in my bones that you are pining for a decent long one, just as much as I was before I got your 1, 2 and 3 – so the least I can do in the way of a Xmas present is this! By the time I finish this letter I hope to be able to include some snaps for you – but that is in the lap of the Gods at the moment.

As I write the guns are banging away, and the R.A.F. are zooming over on another low altitude blitz, and the dust is just about coming up for its afternoon blow. Fortunately, now it's a bit cooler, even during the day, as the winter is really coming on now, and we'll be looking out our battle-dress soon. The desert is the same as ever – too, too depressing – but we've not too much time to be 'browned off' right now – there's a big job to be done, and it has to be done for next Spring, so we're told – then we can come home and help Ham's lot I expect!! I'd rather do that job than this one, anyhow – you have to fight against the conditions *as well* here!!! and they're atrocious. As I've said to you before, we'll all come out of this desert better men, and certainly more appreciative of home comforts. There's nothing I'd like so much as to have a clean meal off clean plates with a real white tablecloth and a good hot bath and a sit by the fire with my feet up, as per usual!! I expect the marks are on the mantelpiece yet, are they? Would that I could add a few more soon!! It's the little bits of comfort and cleanliness that we all miss more I think than the fact that we're so far from home. What I mean is that it has to be faced but if condi-tions could be a bit better it would be easier for us to bear the separation. I definitely dislike having half an inch of sand at the foot of my cup of tea – one of the Kintore spreads seems like Paradise compared to eating out of the eternal mess-tin and gulping down ones food before the flies can do their worst on it. (Literally!!) Still I am getting steadily more used to the crudity of life as time goes on – I find myself only worried about little things, like scratches that fester and tea being cold, and being occas-ionally constipated. But that is because all our interests revolve about our-selves, there being no outside interest or attraction whatever. In this respect we are almost like the bed-ridden invalid whose one thought is himself.

You must excuse this beastly pencil but then my pen is smashed, and until you can send me one, as I asked you in an airgraph – then I am lost!! There is no possible hope of getting one here, as the ration trucks that come up have to be filled to the doors with bully and beans and things – no one bothers about sending up effeminacies like pens and ink, which to

Example of the letter cards provided
for prisoners of war in Germany.

Kriegsgefangenenpost

GEPRÜFT
56

An Mrs K M BALL

~~WOOLCOMBE~~
166 Hagley Rd.
Empfangsort: SAMPFORD ARUNDEL
Straße: NR TAUNTON
Kreis: SOMERSET
Land: ENGLAND.
Landesteil (Provinz usw.):
BIRMINGHAM

PASSED
P.W. 2428

EDGBAS
 führenfrei

Deutschland (Allemagne)

Lager-Bezeichnung: M.-Stammlager Luft 3
Gefangenennummer:
Vor- und Zuname: F/Lt G. F. BALL No 89401
Absender:

March

June 9/44.

2.

29/3/44. My dear Mummy. I'm longing to
hear from you, and that you are well and the
Y.W. and everything is going strong. I expect you
have supplanted this Curwen by now. I'm limited
to 3 letters & 4 P.C.s a month, I'm writing to Boy now
but I will save the rest of the letters for you. But
please there is no limit on how many letters I may
receive. Can you get the gen from the Red Cross on
Parcels etc. I'm allowed a uniform parcel & 1 clothing
parcel every 3 months. Can you please send the best
of my uniform, as I shall have to get a new uniform
anyway when I get back. You can make up the weight in
the clothing parcel with chocolate. The things I need in
rough order of priority, Uniform Parcel: Tunic, Trousers, Shoes, Tie,
Forage Cap, Shirts (collar attached please), Pullover. Clothing Parcel:
Pyjamas, Shaving Brush, Tooth paste, Razor Blades, Tooth Brush,
Pipe, Pipe cleaners, Comb, Nail Brush, Gym shoes, Socks, Handkerchiefs,

under clothes, Towel. Shirts, (collar attached). Can you also please
place a standing order for a 1,000. cigs (Players. Duty free)
and 2 lbs of Tobacco (Balkan Sobranie) to be sent out each
month. Parcels don't always get through so could you please
send a 1,000 cigs & 2 lbs Tobacco weekly for the first 2
months, we are mutual account for debts and please draw
as much as you want for yourself I would much rather you used it. L f. G.

my mind are just as important to the soldier's happiness in the desert...

The Jocks are behaving magnificently – cheery under all circs. – singing and whistling and cracking the old, old jokes. Nothing will ever damp their spirits, so when I occasionally feel a bit low they soon cheer me up with cries of "Look at Mr. Morrison – he must have had his leave cancelled" or something equally fatuous, but it serves, it serves!! Life here reaches a very elementary stage in which the necessities are: (1) Food (2) Latrines (3) A bivvy or funk-hole (4) Clean weapons (5) Mail – and the fourth is the most most difficult of all for the sand penetrates *everywhere*, and all the guns and rifles have to be cleaned two or three times every day or they simply won't fire, and that's that!!

The mornings and evenings here are delicious – there are no flies, and the skies are wonderful shades and colours of sunrise and sunset – and the stars are so bright you can nearly read by their light. When we travel, it's nearly always at night, and by the stars – like all the ancient mariners did before us. The desert is very like the sea in lots of ways – so flat, so immense, and so easy to get lost in if you don't watch your compass, and map like a hawk. If I ever was a crack hand at a compass, I'm doubly so now – it's vital here, even for a visit to a neighbouring platoon or Company, as we are all so dispersed that we hardly ever see anyone but my own wee 32 men, and a grand bunch they are. My platoon cook, Ballingall, from Leslie, Fife, is a wizard – he turns out rissoles, omelettes, rice puddings, steaks and scones with an energy that amazes me. He has an oven, constructed out of a bit of a German tank and makes us all sorts of dainties on the most unappetizing looking rations which come in with the water and the mail every day. Each man gets $1\frac{1}{4}$gals. of water per day for all purposes, i.e. cooking, washing, and shaving, and washing his clothes – not much I assure you. It works out that you get about 1 pint to drink as such, one pint to wash, shave and wash clothes in and the rest for cooking – i.e. tea, stews, potatoes, etc. The rations are surprisingly good – all canned of course, meat doesn't keep more than a few hours in this place – mostly Australian stuff – beans, sausages, tomatoes, oranges, meat, potatoes, rice, flour, salt, sugar and tea are about all I can think of at the moment. We occasionally see some Australian or South African beer – but it is sorry stuff compared to any local brew in Scotland – not that I miss it in the least – to get drunk here would be suicide, that's all!! This active service business isn't bad at all, you know – there's an immense amount of kit and supplies pouring in from Britain and we lack for nothing in that line. That's why I think this coming winter should see the Nazis out of Egypt *and* Libya – for their supplies are running dangerously low (for them!) Everyone in the 8th. Army is most cheerful about the outcome, regardless of past misfortunes, and I must say I feel that very very strongly too. We see no newspapers of course, but I expect they verify that hope of ours...

The mail business Unfortunately, the mail only comes in blocks of three or four, as far as I can see, with long gaps in between – I suppose as each convoy comes in – so we'll never really get in decent contact that way. The only way I can see is for you to send me an Air letter – i.e. ordinary letter with "By Air Mail" blue stamp – or alternatively – airgraphs – you can get some forms at the P.O. – or "Air Letter Cards" like I send you or E.F.M's – i.e. Expeditionary Force Messages – that's the three phrases for

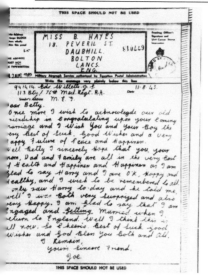

Air graph letter cards such as this one were designed to overcome the shortage of transport aircraft available to carry mails to and from the fighting fronts. By means of micro-photography, these letter cards could be produced in miniature and a hundred or more could be sent and put into the space that would ordinarily be required for one letter.

2/6 or something, – or N.L.T's which are marvellous. I unfortunately can't afford to send you more than one in a blue moon – because they're 10/6d a crack, and I have to wait a few weeks at a time before I get my pay from the field cashier – but there you are!! Pick your choose and send bags of it – carry on with the ordinary letter though, every week – because they'll all catch up with me some time or other, and even if it's months old – a letter from you could never be stale, when written in the inimitable Noni style. I almost cried when I got your 1, 2 and 3 the other day – it reminded me so strongly of all I hold dear – it took me right back to that wee house of ours, and in amongst the folk with all the blethers and non-sense and gossip and fun and worry and invalids and things. I tell you – it was the best thing that's happened in my young life, so far!! I can't possibly hope to tell you all mail means here – but 1st. let me thank you at least for putting such a lot of stout work into these letters. I know how boring it is to keep writing and not hearing – but it's well worth it, in the long run.

I wrote a good few letters on the boat, which you should have by this time, posted probably en route in one of the ports of call. I know from your NLT that seven air letters have got to you, so probably some from here are with you now. I just wish yours would be as quick. Mail → here is much slower than mail → you – queer, but there you are!! It's funny to think that by the time you read this – the fire will be on, and probably it will be raining like hell outside, with the wind whistling round the house. I'm sitting in a hole 6′ by 5′ by 5′ deep with a truck tarpaulin over the top, sitting on a canned bean box at ten to two with the flies around so thick I stop every ten words to shoo them away, and the sun lashing down and the sand blowing everywhere, and the sweat coming off me, drip, drip, drip and an odd orderly peching in with a message, and an odd bang or two, and an odd whine or two – and me – stripped to the waist with an old tin pot on me head and my desert boots with their 1″ thick rubber soles, and my shorts from Dugan & Mitchell, Aberdeen, and my shirt hanging up on the floor beside me – I can just see the two pips having a peek at me, from here – and all my equipment ready to put on at a moment's notice, and my valise outside, ditto. – and all round the wee funk holes – or slit trenches where all the Jocks are writing their letters or eating some buckshee rations or smoking, or just sweating – we may be here five minutes or may be five days, who knows – we don't, nor do we care. Further away, in another biggish hole like mine, squats Ballingall the cook – conjuring up a meal for 32 men and an officer out of grubby tins of rations – a petrol tin full of sand with holes in the sides, the sand soaked in petrol and lit – The Benghazi Cooker to unit – and a few filthy knives and ladles – and an exquisite meal will be brought me in an hour or so by my batman in my slightly soiled mess tin, which I will eat with gusto, as usual!! That, roughly, is the situation at present, and until a runner comes running along to me with a message which reads – "To OC 12 PL from OC B Coy. Ready to move in 004 minutes" or something, then we're all set for another evening, when I will squat here and play my chanter and the men will all be thinking – why doesn't he shut up and give us some peace to think of our wee Lizzie in Lochgelly instead of being a pest at this time of night – But I am indefatigable – I play on until my eyes begin to pop and then

An NCO of the Staffordshire Yeomanry frying fish cakes in the Western Desert, October 1942.

I stop, have a carefully shaded smoke, and then removing the boots, desert pairs one, and nothing else, clamber or crawl or otherwise insinuate myself into ye olde greene sleeping bagge – which you paid for so long ago in Perth when I was rookie, remember? Little did I think, etc.——!!!

Now, what in God's name can I give you in the way of news when this is the state of affairs? I ask you, I ask you!! Still, I am determined that this shall be a very prince of letters – a sine qua non – a masterpiece – in other words, something which you may hand round from hand to hand, and say in a hushed and reverential voice – "This, this my friends is from my boy at the Front" – at the Front I repeat, – one of the country's heroes, who sweats that we may live, who goes to the bathroom in a bully beef tin and buries it, that we may use our Shanks Patent Flush – who lives with scorpions, snakes, lizards, flies and desert rats which sometimes attain to a length of nine inches, that we may live to complain bitterly of a mouse in the attic mayhap, or a weed in the garden – who eats on an average two lbs. of sand a day that we may be safe in saying that the sugar is filthy this week – etc. etc. etc. etc.!!!! End quote, and about time!! OK?

OK!! OK!! OK!! When I get home – I repeat, when I get home, I'll probably eat squatting in the lobby, imploring you to throw some dirt on the food so that I can eat it!! Then, when all is done, I'll crawl on all fours into the gas cupboard under the stairs and there smoke a furtive cigarette, jumping three inches every time GP coughs (as if I never did before!!) and curl finally under the pantry sink and go peacefully to sleep, no matter what time of day it is!! That's one art I've learnt, and a very valuable one it is too – keeps you going great stuff. But – it's not so bad as all that, Noni, – it's me trying to be funny I think!! I'm in great fettle to-day – just got an NLT from you saying you're glad I've got some mail – I'm glad you're glad I'm glad.

Later

A typical thing has just happened – I've suddenly and for no particular reason just been away out in a tank for a recci. – bumping over miles of scrubby sand and sandy scrub, and here I am again in the same wee hole, writing the same enormous letter. You'll notice that I've now got the MO's paper and things are definitely more refined-looking now!! But I am even more dusty and travel stained, – but just as full of cheer, the better for meeting some real nice Aussies – great bunch they are and they get on better with us than any of these English regiments – and say so. The Aussie's never a man to mince his words – take it from me!!

*

20th. September (Sunday morning)

And so, Sunday has come round again – not that it makes much odds, you know, but still, Sunday is Sunday I suppose. I think of you all busily getting ready for the kirk – how remote, how far off!!

You know, this letter is coming on famously, the champion of my long epistolary career!! – My cook has just brought me in a mug of really good army tea – thick and stewed and very sustaining to carry me on through the murky mass of pages yet to be written!!. . .

You know, Mother, the thing that gets me just every so often is – here am I frittering away my life in the Egyptian desert, probably shortening my life by several years, and the sand I'm inhaling and imbibing – when I could be getting on with my life's work, and should be. But then, there are so many like me that I can't mean too much – but what a bloody waste of time all this war business is!!

"Would you be a lamb and run down to McCartneys for the scones for the tea?" "Can I take your bike, Mother?" "Certainly not" – and I did too!! – My, how it makes me wild, just to think of all I'm missing, and all the other lads with me!!! Well the sooner we finish this off – the sooner we'll be running for the scones and taking our dirty feet off the mantelpiece, and writing to A.J. when we would, and climbing these big braes again!!

If you're in Moncurs any time – tell the wee man that cut my hair, where I am – he was out in the M.E. last War – Gallipoli I think, or one of these places, but I'll bet he would be tickled to think I was here!!

I think you'll be pretty fed up of this letter by this time – should I stop? No? All right, – you asked for it!! Whether I'll get it all in one envelope remains to be seen!! I don't think all the same that, I can wait until the

A sergeant writes home from North Africa, October 1942.

photos come back from Cairo, or you'll be getting a book, not a letter!!

I hope you understand my life here better now – I can spread my feelings a bit better in a letter and give you a more complete story, but I'll carry on with Air letters as I've said and throw an odd one of these in when I have time. I'll send the photos on about the 25th or so, when they come back and I'll try to do a few more pages for then. Not, mind you, that its a strain, or a bother – you're the one person on earth that understands my peculiar personality, and you're the one person I have the most respect and love for of all others, and so it is right that I should tell you everything I can about me and my problems, for if you can't understand me, no one can, least of all myself! I never fully appreciated your qualities when I was younger, but I am older & wiser, I hope I can see what a fortunate man I am to have such a splendid soul for a Mother. Brushing aside all sentimentality, which I abhor, or think I do, if it wasn't for the thought that you were at home, waiting for me to come back, praying for me perhaps, and certainly thinking of me, then I would be undone – no more, no less. So for God's sake look after yourself and keep the old grin on your face – and I'll be back to worry you a bit more in no time!!

So – give my love to Granny and tell her not to eat things she didn't ought – to Grandpa and tell him to take care of wee Peter – to Winifred and tell her to take care of you and be the buffer state as usual and to burnish up her cooking for I'll be hungry when I get back – to Winnie and Ham and tell them to tell wee Elspeth that her Uncle Geo (Uncle *not* cousin – I refuse to be that) will be back to teach her how to swear – to

Mrs. L. my old sparring partner and tell her to sharpen up the tongue for a few more lively encounters on my return; to KML and tell him to remember not to swot too hard – to A.J. my love and wish all the old folk my congratulations on being ages they are. I'll never be their age!! I don't know if I've missed anyone out. Tell Mrs. McLaggar I wish her all the best – tell Miss Lowson I thank her for her good wishes and return them, tell the Halleys and the Diaks I'm asking for them, and the Sellars and the Hutsons – tell wee Peter I'll give him at least *one* real walk when I get back – if I can be bothered!! And for yourself, keep an eye on that front gate and if you see a taxi rolling up with a dusty valise on the back grid and a sunburnt George in the back, with German helmets, pistols and things dangling in all directions you'll know the day has come when all this nonsense is over, and I can be once more in the bosom of my family and quietly vegetate for awhile before rushing off again to do something daft or other!

All my love to you, Mother – keep writing and keep smiling and God Bless you all.

George.

———

November 1942

My Darling,

When I was walking back from Heyford station yesterday, I realised how little I appreciated the beauty of the countryside, how little I seemed to take interest, and on realising that, I stopped on the road and looked about me, and for the first time noticed how lovely everything is about here.

Having found that out, I tried to fathom the question of why I hadn't noticed it before, why I wasn't taking my usual interest in the countryside, for although I'm not of poetic nature or anything like it, I feel that I've always taken quite a lot of interest in my surroundings. I loved the Isle of Wight and all places of natural beauty, especially St. Martha's which holds such wonderful memories for me.

And I came to these conclusions.

Firstly, this beastly war. War has no rightful place on this earth, besides destroying men and property, everything that is seen, it destroys those unseen things, ourselves, our sense of beauty, happiness, comradeship amongst all men, everything that is worth living for. Property is not essential, but happiness, a love of beauty, friendship between all peoples and individuals is life itself.

Secondly, you. I've put you second. I wonder if you feel that strange. But this affects everybody. I'd be very selfish if I put you first in this thought I'm trying to fathom out for myself. You are just everything to me. The unforgivable way I write would make another feel that you have been guilty of my loss in taking no notice in the surrounding beauty, but you understand, I'm sure, that it is only because I'm not constantly with you, that is the real factor. You, Darling, have made me able to see, to feel and to understand all the beauty that is in the world and life itself. Without you that understanding does not disappear, for you are with me constantly in my thoughts, but that understanding of life does seem to fade.

Flight Lieutenant L.E. Stockwell served as a pilot with Pathfinder Force, Bomber Command, R.A.F., and was killed on a mission in January 1943. This letter was written to his wife.

This war is keeping us apart, and therefore it is to blame in my loss, and that loss is not only mine but of every person in the world connected with this war.

I have never spoken to you of my feelings and thoughts about this war, and I hope will never speak of them again. Do you remember a small boy saying he would be a conscientious objector if war came? Things happened to change that small boy's views, talk of brutality, human suffering, atrocities, but these did not have any great effect on changing my views for I realise that we are all capable of doing these deeds of which we read so much nowadays.

It is the fact that a few people wish to take freedom from the peoples of the earth that changed my views. News of atrocities only breeds hate, and hate is contemptable in my eyes. I will never be capable I hope of hating anyone whatever they have done.

Why should I then fight in this war which only brings disgust into my thoughts?

It is so that I might live in happiness and peace all my days with you. You notice I put myself first, again it is a strange thing, but I am trying hard to be honest with myself and I find that I, and consequently everybody, am terribly selfish, it is human nature.

I am also fighting so that one day happiness will again rule the world, and with happiness that love of beauty, of life, contentment, fellowship among all men may return.

You may again have noticed that I have not mentioned fighting for one's country, for the Empire, that to me is just foolishness, for greatness in one nation will always breed hate and longing in another, and the whole of life will again be disrupted.

Mainly, however, I'm fighting for freedom of all men, and in that I am fighting just as much for the German as for the English people.

With freedom and the destruction of hate this world will enter into a period which I hope will be much in advance of anything it has ever known.

When peace returns, and may it be soon, the world must make sure that the men and women of the future are educated in the right way, a love of beauty not a love of war, and it is our own job to teach our children about all the lovliness of this world, to make them happy so that they can understand that love and happiness are the things really worth having.

Well Darling, I seem to have been rambling on for some time, really I must stop. I don't know whether I have made any sense out of my ramblings, I only hope so.

Todays news is very small. I saw "They flew alone" tonight, and I think I enjoyed it, I'm not quite sure.

"The Stars look down" although not a pleasant sort of book has held my interest and I'm reading solidly through it.

All my love Darling, you mean so very much to me,

Always,

Lancie.

———

At the time of writing this letter Christopher Milner was a captain in the Rifle Brigade, serving as a Staff Officer with the 22nd Armoured Brigade in the Western Desert.

Christopher Milner's photograph of General Montgomery.

Started 31st December, 1942

Dear M & D,

The end of 1942. What a year! Elgar's "Pomp and Circumstance" being played. 95,000 and 72,000 at Stalingrad* is the news from Russia.

It is Hogmany and there are two Scots in the Mess. "A special review of the Past Year" over the air. The Colonel has just ordered a "Hot Mrassas" for us all – hot lime juice and whiskey that is. At the main table poker is going on in rollicking style. I've just finished reading Thomas Mann's "The Coming Victory of Democracy" – thanks to Donald.

I took Pat Fitzgerald over to "A" Company to have a drink before dinner – Teddy Garnier is now a major and commanding it; many old friends were there and in great form. There is still the memory of Monty's visit yesterday – talking to everyone, pulling the legs of the "blackbuttons"†. Gazelle for supper again.

Out tomorrow to watch a sqaudron shooting – but that will be 1943 won't it? Donald will soon be 20. I shall be 23. You will be – ? But it does'nt matter. You must be feeling happier now than you did when we were at Alamein, before the Russians began their onslaught, when things in England must have been most unpleasant . . . . . .

After writing this I wrapped my greatcoat round myself even more tightly, put my feet up on a chair, with the knob of the wireless set within easy reach in case the Poker School was not in sympathy with the programme I had selected (their moods changed with their fortunes) and snoozed the time away until we felt that it was somewhere soon after midnight. I was not feeling in the least like Auld Lang Syne but eventually participated in the toasts and the singing in of the New Year. All were satisfied but the two Scotsmen. A poor Hogmany they said. No haggis. No snow or rain. They must wait until it was 1943 in Glasgow – an hour and a half to go – before they could end their vigil in peace. So we left them to it.

The General Montgomery came to lunch with us a few days ago. He has a remarkable gift for talking to anyone at any length on almost any subject. On going the rounds of a unit he seldom asks the same question twice; often raises a laugh. His own idiosyncracy is that he repeats himself, to give greater emphasis and yet in part as though he were thinking it over to himself. "You're a Scot? Ha-Ha-a Scot? You're a savage then. Yes, you're a savage. A savage." And everyone roars with laughter, since I do'nt think he does it on purpose. Another was:- "I told them to go". Pause. "Yes, I told them to go." Pause again. "– and they've gone!"

He loves to let people take his photograph. The Brigadier's driver asked if he could, and General drew himself up, "click" went the camera, but instead of moving on he said "What! only one?" and the driver's mate said that he would like to take one too. I snapped him as he was putting his coat on and he was quite disappointed that I was not anxious to take a real "still". He even had the sauce to remark that the Middle East was run by the Green Jackets when he arrived – "All the promotions committees run by blackbuttons" chipped in the Brigadier. In self-defence I murmured

*Dead and prisoners.

†black buttons – nickname for the Rifle Regiments.

"They've nearly been exterminated now, Sir" which M. luckily thought to be "They're nearly extinct now Sir" which was a deal more tactful than my original statement. I must admit that at one time there were a lot of people from the 60th. and the Rifle Brigade holding important offices. But then we each have several battalions out here.

I had a couple of flights in an old Bombay transport plane yesterday. On a demonstration which took us out to a newly constructed desert aerodrome. I found a copy of a thing called "True Confessions" to read, which kept my mind away from the bumping of the machine, even though the subject matters was deplorable. Glad I did too, because the two gentlemen on my left had to stagger to the rear for a breath of fresh air.

I still cannot overcome my aversion to the RAF tendency to disregard turnout and shaving in the desert, but they certainly deliver the goods when it comes to doing the job – as we found especially when we were coming back through Tobruk along the main road after the Knightsbridge battles, packed nose to tail yet not a single Boche plane did they allow over to attack us. That was only one good thing for which we are grateful.

Could you find and send me a copy of the Pocket Oxford Dictionary? Should be one belonging to me in the house. Also thank Ted heartily for his telegram of New Year greetings. The enclosed cheque is for Naval or Merchant Marine charity. Donald may be able to recommend one.

Much Love
C.F.

———

R A F April 1943

Flying Officer Jack Yeoman was a navigator in 218 Squadron, Bomber Command, R.A.F. He was killed on the night of 12/13 September 1943 when his aircraft was shot down on a raid over Germany. Stella O'Hare, the woman he wrote to, dreamed of his fate that night. The letter was forwarded to her after his death; it had been written five months earlier.

Stella Darling,
This is a letter written despite our decision not to write again – it is a letter I hope you will never receive because it will only be sent to you if I am killed, posted as missing or something equally final.

This, especially put as such a bold statement, will probably be a most unpleasant shock to you. I am very sorry about that, but there are one or two things I want to tell you which will hardly be breaking our agreement as I shall have ceased to be the Jack you knew and loved.

I feel somehow that our decision not to marry is now justified. You have at least been spared a lot of anxiety you would otherwise have had, even though it has been at the cost of the happiness I know we would have enjoyed together.

Hundreds of times since we said goodbye I have felt I had been an idiot, that I was needlessly torturing myself and you too, my darling – that we should have married in March and hang the consequences, let the future take care of itself, leave the problems of family and education until the question arose, that we should treat ourselves to the happiness of each other's company and live only in the present.

Now that this has happened, maybe you will agree I was right in Reeces* that first time we went out to lunch together. Now you are still free and have no family to hinder the future of a young girl alone in a world where everyone will be fighting for jobs and livelihoods. You may for all I know

*Reeces Lyceum Cafe in Liverpool.

Jack Yeoman and Stella O'Hare.

be married. If so, I hope your husband is worthy of you and that he appreci-
ates what a real treasure he has for a wife. I envy him and I hope – I sincerely
and genuinely hope – you will be happy.

On the other hand, you may not be married – perhaps it is more than
likely you are not. I can't, of course, know now as I write when I shall
meet the fate that will send this letter on to you. . . . .

For myself, I have few regrets and have never regretted joining the RAF.
I only hope I have got a few cracks at the Hun or Jap before meeting my
own end and that I am killed while engaged on an operation and not just
run down by a bus or crashing on a practice flight or something equally
unexciting. But as far as the possibility of death is concerned, I am a complete fatalist; nor strangely enough, am I particularly worried or scared
about the possibility. I can say honestly, while I like living with a fervour
I perhaps never show very obviously, the prospect of an early finish to my
life, which this job must of necessity entail, has never held any terrors for
me.

You may find this strange in a barbarian such as I since I do not rely
on any thoughts of peace or comfort in an hereafter. To my way of thinking,
I cease to be at the moment of biological death – that little good I may
have done may live on in someone's memory, but for the time being I was,
I can conceive of no future.

To you, my darling Stella, I am grateful for having loved me. You can
have no idea what that has meant to me.

For as long as I can remember, I have been a quiet, unassuming non-
entity, seeking refuge in work and on the whole being reasonably successful
at it, whether at school or in the RAF. To some extent, that success has
been its own reward, but I have never been the life of the party. The few
people who knew me well have, I feel, been very fond of me – but you
were more than just "fond' . . . you wanted to have me with you always,
to share everything, including yourself, with me, and for that I cannot
easily express my gratitude.

Whether or not we were wise at the time may be a debatable point. Deliberately to cause ourselves so much pain seems very foolish, yet I find myself glad to think we did agree to part now that this has happened.

However big a shock my death is to you now, it is nothing compared with what it would have been had we been married. I have wondered whether I ought to reopen old wounds by writing this letter at all, but I can't bear the idea of your hearing of this casually in a newspaper. . . .

Despite our decision not to write or see each other, to me you have always been the girl I love, I often re-live our all too short time together. If you knew how much your photo has meant to me, you would never have regretted the agony of having it taken.

Well, my sweetheart, there is so little and yet so much left for me to say.

Don't, above all, let our having loved one another interfere in any way with your own future – that would be breaking a solemn promise. It was only with the genuine hope that you would not suffer from our friendship that I believe we were right to call it off.

In a way, I wish I could have seen your point of view on religion, but that – and I think you understood fully – was quite impossible, even when it meant losing you. And knowing how much your religion meant to you, I would never have expected you to change it. I would have been a very poor substitute for your faith. . . .

I only hope you will find someone who will love and cherish you as I would have and who can also share your religion with you as a belief as sincere as yours should be shared. If so, everything will have been worth-while and our decision more than justified. For myself, I have done what I know at least to be right, just in joining the war of my own free will and giving up a chance of supreme happiness with you. What more can anyone ask?

So this is my final goodbye. Thank you once more, my darling, for your love and may God bless you and grant you the success and peace in your life to come which you so richly deserve.

My love goes with you always.

Jack.

––––––––

Sergeant Edward Cope served with the 2nd Battalion, the Rifle Brigade, in the Middle East. This letter was written to his fiancée. Doreen and Edward were eventually married in the spring of 1945.

6915914 Sgt.E.Cope.M.M.
'S' Coy. 2nd. Bn. Rifle Bde.
M.E.F.
5th. July '43

Dear Doreen,

I've just received your letters 20 and 21, which means that once again there are none missing, although 21 did reach me after 20. And its mainly of the latter one that I want to write about. Do you remember it was written in answer to my 'down in the dumps' letter. I've read it about 6 times already, and I only received it yesterday afternoon – so, whether you know or not, it certainly is a very special letter for me.

I certainly was in the dumps when I wrote that other letter to you, and yet I knew that, unless I did write it, I could never write sincerely again.

L915914 L/Cpl. Cope E.,
2 Pln. 'A' Coy, 2nd Bn. R.B.
M.E.F.
9th April, 42.

Dear Doreen,

Time goes by with such a sameness nowadays that it is difficult to remember the date, the day and even the month. On two successive Sundays recently it has been evening before I've realised that it was Sunday. I trust that the maxim – 'a Sabbath well spent brings a week of content, etc.' – only has effect providing you know that you are working on a Sunday.

Spring no doubt is with you now and all the trees and shrubs are showing green. The bicycle will probably have had a thorough overhaul and will certainly be on active service by the time this letter reaches you!

It must be the Spring out here too that has affected the lower orders of animal life (not too low!). Small lizards are quite common; the day before yesterday we caught a small chameleon and yesterday a small tortoise came dashing up to us. That probably will surprise you, but he certainly did move. They all live on insects and there are plenty of those about.

How goes the star-gazing? With every day a sunny day and every night star-lit, it is easy for us to be interested especially when they are in the only roof over our head (see R.L. Stevenson's poem). For about three nights last week the moon had a halo, not small as I've seen in England, but of radius the length of Orion!

Mentioning R.L. Stevenson's poem; by the way, I believe its the Epitaph; reminded me that the other week I came across a poem by G.K. Chesterton that I haven't heard since Fred learnt it at school, about 17 years ago. Its a lovely little poem and strangely appropriate in title – 'The Ass'! I read another of his at the same time, and that also is really very fine, true and amusing – 'The Rolling English Road'. They both are really worth reading; if you mention the first one to Fred I'm sure he'll remember it – I think his form-master then was Mr. Ascot.

Have you been to any more shows? The English climate will probably make it preferable to stay indoors at night for two or three weeks more, until May comes in, and then you'll probably have a real scorching summer to make up for last winter!

Has Aunt Tom planned out the garden with Lunch's aid? No doubt Mr. Broxford's garden already looks a treat, unless all his spare time has been taken up mending burst water pipes!

I'm waiting at the moment for another letter from Fred to hear how Gladys and Dad are getting on. In fact it is nearly three weeks since I had a letter from anyone. Still that means I should be getting some soon!

One of Edward Cope's letters written on the air mail letter card available to troops.

BY AIR MAIL

AIR MAIL LETTER CARD

IF ANYTHING IS ENCLOSED THIS CARD WILL BE SENT BY ORDINARY MAIL

POSTAGE REVENUE 3D

PASSED BY CENSOR NO. 1841

Miss D. Roots,
1, Morton Road,
Morden,
Surrey.

ENGLAND.

WHEN FOLDED THE LETTER CARD MUST CONFORM IN SIZE AND SHAPE WITH THE BLUE BORDER WITHIN WHICH THE ADDRESS ONLY MAY BE WRITTEN.

Does that sound peculiar? In your letter you say that you do not get your thoughts down as clearly as I; well (in a very 'umble way, as Uriah Heep would say) I beg to differ. For whereas your letters are quite clear, I find, when I re-read mine, that they get so involved that sorting the ideas out is quite a job. I can find only one suggestion to explain this, and that is that what we write is our true thoughts, which as soon as expressed become incomprehensible to ourselves or nearly so, but at the same time quite clear to the other. Anyway it would be an interesting theory to work out.

But apart from the theory, quite apart from it, every now and again in your letters you say something especially sweet and it makes me realise just how much I am in love with you. I am always thinking and dreaming of you and our future life.

That there should be a war is unfortunate, but to me it is not a total evil. For all the pain and misery and death, there is still the balance of strengthening, of endurance, of tempering of character and temperance in outlook, and always striving for something better, and the final contentment in all the little pleasures of life, unheeded before.

Am I preaching now? as you accused yourself in your letter. Perhaps I am, but what I am really trying to express, is my love for you, that you are my whole life, and that, just as you are waiting so am I, impatiently perhaps, but at least contented in the faith that you will be there when I return to start life anew.

Isn't it peculiar to have an interlude in one's life of four or more years; and yet the end always seems just around the corner. I'm sure that we in this war, I mean all the young people, will never grow mentally old. Perhaps its not so obvious in civvy street, but it seems especially noticeable in the army, where chaps from 20 to 40 act and play quite naturally like schoolboys. Its a youthfulness that I'm sure will always remain stamped in their character, and will come obvious in violent outbursts of schoolboy pranks when any group of them get together again!!

In your letter you say you weren't sure, whether or not, to let me know that you had got some things for our home. Well I'm awfully glad you did, for few things could interest me more. Can I help in getting things for our home? You see, I have authorised Fred to draw on my bank account and he could always draw whatever you wanted, if at any time you should see anything that you would like. Pop and your mother would be your most reliable guides as to what is worth getting now, for no doubt after this war, as after the last, prices will be high for a few years.

Give my love to all and tell Win I hope she has recovered from her toothache.

Well, cheerio for now, my darling,

All my love

Ted

P.S. If you should have such unluck as to be awake at 0530hrs. in the morning, just let the thought pass through your mind that we go swimming in the sea at that time every morning. Its a lot more pleasant than it sounds, though, especially out here – that is apart from the getting up (still even this is left to the very last minute!)

———

The next letter was written by Major Lionel Wigram who served with the 5th Battalion, East Kent Regiment ('The Buffs') and at the time of writing this letter was attached to the 6th Battalion, Royal West Kent Regiment. Major Wigram was killed in action on 3 February 1944 while leading a party of Italian irregulars behind the German lines; he was shot by a sniper.

6   R.W.K. Rgmt.
C.M.F.
[undated]

My darling babe,

I have just received your letter of the 26th telling me all about Michael's birthday party and it has put me in a cheerful frame of mind for the rest of the day. I suppose there must be several other letters addressed to the Buffs which I just haven't received yet and which I am going to chase up today if I get the chance.

I am very well in spite of the tough life we are leading now (or perhaps because of it). It is a very simple life in which things like food and comfort assume ridiculous proportions. For instance "scrounging" – means the ability to move around and supplement the ration. We have done extremely well in this respect – bread, chickens, sheep a pig even geese and a few eggs. All this makes life well worth living and there is a tremendous sense of satisfaction to be gained out of seeing the men eat with gusto.

It is a weird life in many ways. We keep driving the Germans before us and often catch them up. The result is that we find ourselves billeted in farms which they have just hurriedly vacated. Imagine the situation. For two or three weeks about 30 Germans have been lording it in a farm. They have turned out the family (23 including many little children) and made them live in a cow barn. Every day they eat all they want – kill chickens, cows, and pigs without paying – and drink all the farmer's vino. They even fill lorries with food and drive them off to the rear. If there is any protest from the farmer or his family out come the revolvers. Then one never to be forgotten night the German sentry on duty at the gate comes running up about midnight "The English"! The English! There is a hasty gathering of kit, shots ring out out in the darkness, the family cower down low in their stable the children yelling and screaming at all the strange noises, then at last off go the Germans up into the hills, on foot, running for life. Quite alot of them don't get away.

Out come the family – and what a welcome we receive! We have the greatest difficulty in stopping them from embracing us. All the women are crying and when we later march through a small village the entire population turns out cheering and screaming. If we go through a town it is the same – just like a ticker tape reception down Broadway. They then produce home made Union Jacks usually green and upside down. It makes you feel a hell of a hero. What a welcome we shall get when we reach countries which are really liberated.

I think of you all the time. I have much more time to think now. If I had the letter cards I should write you a letter every day and tell you how beautiful you are. Perhaps it is just well I haven't.

Many happy returns my dear darling and love to all my babies.

xxx   x   xxxxxxxxxxx
Daddie

———

Bill and John Smith were brothers, serving in the Cheshire Regiment and the Royal Engineers respectively. Bill's letter of 1941 was written from the Middle East. John writes home from North Africa in 1943; but, by this time, Bill had been killed in action eleven months earlier (on 12 July 1942) and neither John nor his parents knew this.

Dear Mother & Father,

I started this letter over a month ago but I never had time to finish it I been so busy. I been quite worried over my hair it made me feel alot older but its not to bad now I think its alot thicker than it was in England. Did you ever hear from a girl in Cuchlington if you did dont take any notice of her I think she's a bit silly I wrote and told her off she said I was supposed to be engaged to her. I've told her to send you my photos back I dont suppose she will she says every morning she gets up she looks at my photo and it gives her courage to go through the day so I told her to send them back and stay in bed all day, talk about love sick she's mad. If a girl made me mad she did. I showed the lads a few of her letters they asked me was she a writer for the Red Star. I get about ten letters a week from her she must write every day the boys get a good laugh from them, one letter I had from her said I went picking blue bells with her the boys didn't half pull my leg over it. Do you remember me talking to you about Douggie Floyd? Well I lost him now it was like losing my left arm he went in hospital and never came back to us I never been out with anyone else since I been with this outfit . . .

I hope you can understand this letter I am writing it under the starlight just like a cowboy, how is John getting on in your last letter you said he had his toe off is he still in the army I hope he's out you've got enough with me out here but when I get home I will never join the army again I mean they'll never get me again no boss next time it will be the Air Force or the navy or maybe home guard . . .

I hope you don't think I'm working myself to death because I'm not I never work since I've been in the army. Well Dear's I must close I cant make my brain work so I will send all my love   Your loving Son Bill

I will be home for my twenty first birthday so dont forget to get that beer ready

Dear Mother,

I can do very little about Billy as I am an awful long way from Alesc, I have been enquiring about him from different boys from his unit but they are new chaps and don't know him but I will do all I can. I was asking a Nurse yesterday if she had been that way, she had but they have so many cases they can't remember all the names of the boys . . . . So Billy Bell is about again trying to keep out of the forces, it makes my blood boil to hear about him. I have been through two actions and he is lying in ease and comfort, us people out here have to suffer heat and thirst and have our different torments never knowing the minute when your life is going to be – puff out and now we are resting all we have to look forward to is the next job we have to do, don't mention him to me again. I could play his game so could thousand of others, the likes of him isn't very heartening to us out here. Well Mother, how are you and Dad keeping. I am always thinking of you all the time, the other night I lay thinking about when we were all small and Dad telling us those stories and the crowd of us all crying of it, but don't worry it won't be long now until we are all home again then we can give short shifts to the Bells and dodgers who were to damn feared to help their country except for lumping coal about. So cheerio for now and don't worry I'm fine.   Your Loving Son, John

Italian women sorting and stamping Christmas air graph forms, 1943.

Lewis Bull, a private in the Royal Army Service Corps, was attached to an anti-aircraft unit serving with the Eighth Army. At the time of writing this letter to his wife, Anne, and daughter, Deirdre, he was facing the German positions near Monte Cassino, in Italy.

Sunday, Dec. 5th. 1943
(Won't bother to put my best suit on)

My Dear Family and Co.

Here I am again, still knocking about the Italian countryside. It's darn cold here now, with snow on yonder mountains.

I am in my little shack which I have built between-times. I guess you would like to see it, built against the quarry-side. It has a thatched roof, the rafters which I borrowed (in a way)! The laths are a few old kinkey ribs which I took off a certain farm when on the scrounge for a few chickens.

I have a cushion (a car seat) for my bed, a table with Ann and Deirdre's photograph on it, a little lamp which I *bought*, a bit of buckshee grub, and, of course, my old fry-pan and brew-tin which was a treacle tin.

So you see I am quite comfortable and have something like a home to come back to. All of us blokes have similar places. It's the first thing we do, find a place to erect our home.

There are bean stacks here, so some of the boys have made runs into the middle of them like moles. We had some fun one night when one of them caved in on top of them, just like rabbits bolting, you bet!

I like mine best, though, nice and warm. I'm like an old hermit, as there's a young oak close by where I hang my washing. Another thing is, you can't hear the guns so much, or the bombers at night.

We are still amongst the mountains. It's pretty scenery, plenty of oaks and chestnuts, but not like our old trees at home. Mangy, I reckon.

In the valleys are the villages and farms, but they are all a mass of ruins, trees torn in half or burnt by shellfire and bombs, dead donkeys and oxen lying around. Nobody bothers as there's not Ities here. Too near old Jerry.

Further back there's plenty of farmers on their little holdings of about ten acres busy ploughing with their big white oxen. When the wind meets them they seem to stop they go so slow. Two oxen pull two furrows, so you see how light the ground is. The women do the narrowing. They must be tough – carry sacks of maize, use a scythe, dig the ground, clean out ditches.

I went down to a farm yesterday to see if I could get some cider. I did.

They were having a meal. The bloke had a loaf which reminded me of something out of a dustbin. He tore bits off with his dirty hands to give his wife and kids a chunk each, which in turn they dipped in a dish of something or other.

They seemed to enjoy it, although it made me feel a bit sick.

I never thought Italians were so backward. You can see they were the same before the war. Their houses are large stones chucked together, no windows and a mighty cellar under each one in which they keep their cider and animals.

The roads or tracks up these mountains are ten times worse than Court Lodge hill, with drops over the sides of anything from a hundred to a thousand feet.

If you get too near the edge, you either hope there's a tree to hold you up until the breakdown lorry arrives, or else you get your kit out and nip out yourself and somebody pushes the lorry out of the way so as not to hold up convoys.

I have been lucky in that respect, but you may depend we have some

A selection of Christmas greetings, drawn by servicemen in Italy, 1943.

tidy capers. We laugh when we are safe and sound or when we tell each other of our day's or night's adventures.

We don't like it at night, especially when it rains. We set off about 4.30 (musn't travel by day on this road as it is under Jerry's fire). No lights, not even a smoke as we creep along in the pitch dark. Your mate walks alongside just to keep you from going too near the edge, as stones will throw your steering about, but it's not as bad as the desert, where it would sprain your wrist.

We do about twenty miles between ours and Jerry's guns, so we have some excitement when they are pheasant shooting. Glad to get there after eight to ten hours at two miles an hour watching the lorry in front, just like a black shadow. It seems to disappear at times, you wonder where the hell a lorry could go to so quick.

But it's when he goes down a bomb crater or a blown bridge – you belt down after him as there's generally two to four feet of water in the bottom. A proper water splash at times, or wet mud. We still laugh over one night, I got ditched. My mate got out to have a look, I said: "What's she like Jack?" No answer. I shouted again. Still no answer. I went round his side and trod on nothing. Away I went rolling down a mud bank. Got to the bottom, heard a mighty swearing and spluttering. "Jack, are you alive?" I said after I had finished my bit of swearing. Jack said: "I'll let you know when I get the muck out of my eyes" We were plastered, drizzling with rain too. Anyway the other drivers flung ropes down, so up we came to deliver our ammo, that night, after four lorries had pulled mine out.

When we go the other way it's a lot better. The roads are decent towards Naples. Anyway you know we earn our money and corned-beef. But mud! you wouldn't belive it unless you saw it. The mules look as if they're resting on their bellies, and our lorries look as though they've got no wheels, so if we have to get out we are like daintly ladies, afraid of the mud.

I'm damned if I know how the Army has got so far as it has. You drive through clouds sometimes, it's so high up, see other clouds below in the valleys, or our fighters below us. I reckon it's as near heaven as I shall ever get.

By the way I went to church the other week (in a cave). It's surprising how many of us go when we get the chance. I guess it's because many a time we say we can only trust in the Lord on this job.

Makes us wonder why there are wars. They have seen nothing in England and never will I hope. I never knew what destruction and starving was but I do now. I often wish Arthur or Les was with me, you want somebody like yourself.

This time last year we were in the desert near Tobruk. A sand storm blew up smothered our dinner with sand. I gained though, as some of the chaps didn't fancy pork and sand. I was frying up pork for a week after.

Well, it looks as though I have written enough. I must get a bath, caught some rain water in a couple of helmets.

Now Mum, I don't want you to worry as I am O.K. and used to this pleasant life, I even have a little robin to visit me – more like home, especially when I come back at nights feeling a bit homesick. I push open the door (hearse door) and see little Deirdre smiling at me. I guess it's worth it, all these months to be away. I think: "Fancy her, a bit of me – dirty scrappy, bad tempered – I shall have to alter my ways or she won't own me as her Dad." Funny to be called Dad. I shall be as pleased as a bloke who wears a civvy suit.

Well, so long all at home.

See you at next dung-spreading.

Lewis.

––––––––

John Harper-Nelson served as a lieutenant with the 1st Battalion, Royal Fusiliers. His letter was written in Italy from a billet in the Abrizzi village of Castel Fientano, in about March 1944.

1st Battalion Royal Fusiliers
CMF
[Undated]

Darling Margie and Annabel and Kitten and Pop, if you're there yet.

Once again we are off back up again after a short rest. We haven't been more than 4 miles from Jerry for 5 months now. The chief consolation is that it can't go on for ever. I don't know if you knew John Gout in the 10th Battalion – a rather Burmese looking type with a military moustache. He went back as bomb-happy as a coot from our last sector – I think he'll probably be down-graded. The strain was cracking him up for a long time so no one was surprised when he finally went. It's especially sad for him as he wanted to be a regular soldier.

Some bright spark has just produced a bottle of beer. It'll have to be split between four of us but it will help to cheer us on our way. As a further nerve-soother (dutch courage if you like) the local country wine that we find in each farmhouse is a great help, and also, almost more than anything else, letters from home. I suppose its just that link with some kind of sanity that keeps us going. Without it we'd all be jibbering inside of a week. Photographs, too. Those famous piles of snapshots that every soldier collects are another invaluable link with old values and past pleasures. That, I'm sure is why front-line soldiers go for that "Home" type of nostalgic sentiment – also why Forces Favourites and Messages from Home are such popular programmes. We all listen solemnly to messages from Hartlepool just to hear those homely voices saying silly, ordinary things. I suppose in England it seems nearly over. Out here it seems interminable. I was thoroughly disgusted to read in 8th Army News (our own excellent army paper) that seats for the Victory parade were being sold for 20 gns. The racketeering little swine who think we're fighting and dying for their right to make a profit from our victory ought to be shoved up in the line for a week or so. Maybe they'd realize that we'll expect a little more than sophisticated applause from people with 20 guinee seats and cheap Union Jacks.

That sort of thing doesn't make a pleasant reading up here. Sorry to be so angry – but we're rather lible to take the war a little seriously out here. Do write soon.

All my love, darlings and love to all at home,

from
Buddy

––––––––

Joseph Goodlad was serving as a staff sergeant with the 3rd Battalion, Grenadier Guards, in Italy. This letter was written three weeks before he was mortally wounded in 1944 during a mortar attack in the course of the Allied advance on Rome.

No. 2615305 Sgt J. Goodlad
No 4 Coy 3rd Bn
Grenadier Guards
CMF

May 9th 1944

My own Darling Wife & Dream Baby, I.L.Y.
I am O.K. and in the pink and hope that this letter will find my Darlings the same. I have had quite a number of lovely letters from you lately; we found this type writer in a Jerry dugout the other day and so I am trying it out but it seems very strange to me. Still I suppose I will get used to it. Somehow my own sweetheart I dont think it will be very long before we are back together again. The news is wonderful isnt it my sweet. I am forever thinking of your darling Velvet Lips. Seems years and years ago since we were together in our Blue Room. If only I could call back the past I made so many mistakes Dearest One and I am only just realizing it. But I have always been in love with you. I dont suppose you can take it in just how very proud I am of you. Your a girl in a million. How is our baby keeping these days. Is she still as lovely as ever. I can see that we are going to have some grand time when I get back home to you sweetheart. Better even than those which we had before I left England and those were great ones weren't they. Wait until Heather Marcia grows up and I shall be able to tell her of the glorious times her Mummy and Daddy had when they were courting. They were glorious ones weren't they Darling. Just cast your mind back darling to Leverhulme park in the afternoon lazing away in the sunshine. Remember the Red outfit you wore with the million dollar legs encased in black silk net stockings. They were such lovely legs and I had so many ambitions about them. I guess you never thought what used to go on in my head did you precious. You know love I used to get very angry with you sometimes especially when you said you wouldn't kiss me because you always say it spoiled your makeup. You certainly teased me a lot didn't you. Goodness, in those days sweet I was certain I would die if you had married anyone else. And now sweet I laugh at it. Do you think you would ever have married anyone else or would you have been content to wait and hope that Joe Goodlad would come back to you someday? I guess I will never know the answer to that question will I sweet, but you might have finished up as Mrs. George you know that boy who had the car and plenty of money but looked a bit of agawp as they say in Bolton.

Gee, Dorothy my dearest one those were old days old. You see my precious those are the times I think about at nights out here. They are lovely memories my sweet arent they. Still you just wait until our Someday comes along and I am back home with you we will be able to have some even more wonderful times wont we sweet. I love you my darling with all my heart and am only waiting for that day to dawn when I come back to you and I'm going to try and make you the happiest girl in the world. Yes dear I'm going to make up for all the time I have been away from you.

I shall have to carry on in ink. One set of key boards has gone bust on the typewriter. I thought Jerry wouldn't give us something for nothing. Well my own Darling Wife don't ever stop loving me will you. Because

I'm absolutely crazy about you my Dearest One. Give our Marcia a big kiss for me and tell her that her Daddy wants her to say her prayers hard then Jesus will send him home to our Dream baby Marcia and her Mummy soon. Well sweetheart keep your chin up and look after yourself and Heather Marcia for me.

I love you Forever and ever.

PS To my Own Darling Wife   xxxxx
    Mummy and Marcia   xxxxxxxxx   xxxxxx
xxxxxxxxxxxxxxxxxxxxxxxxxxxx   xxxxxxx
                    Yours,
                        Joe

_____

Under the shade of a palm tree in Sicily, a trooper sitting on top of his tank types a letter, August, 1943.

Gerald Ritchie was the captain commanding A Company, 12th (Yorkshire) Battalion, Parachute Regiment, during the Normandy landings. This letter to his sister, written over several days, is an account of his experiences from the time that his aircraft departed for France on the night 5th/6th June 1944 until, after being wounded, he was evacuated to England on 8 June.

Depot and School Airborne Forces
Chesterfield
Derbyshire
Sunday

My dear Muriel,

Thank you so much for your letter received some time ago when I was in hospital, as you see I am now out, thank goodness and am more or less alright again, I've still a bit of a hole in my arm but nothing to speak of. I must say that I was terribly lucky as the bit of shrapnel missed everything important, it went in about four inches below my shoulder, rather on the inside of my arm and stopped just below the surface on the outside of the arm towards the back of it, it missed the bone and didn't do much to the muscles as I could move it about in a few days, and by going round the outside missed all the arteries etc. under the arm, so it might have been a lot worse. They didn't have to dig very deep getting it out either. As you say it was a party which I wouldn't have missed for anything but even though I was only in it for fortyeight hours, and for my lot the first part was, from all accounts, a picnic, compared with the time they had after I left. It all seems rather like a particularly bad dream looking back on it. I expect you would like to hear about the little bit I saw of it so I will start at the beginning. The days before the party started were as you may imagine rather hectic ones, we were cut off from the outside world completely and spent our time going over our little bit of the operation over and over again with maps photos and models, until everyone knew their piece backwards. We enplaned late in evening of the Monday and it all seemed very unreal, it was difficult to imagine that by dawn on the next day, we should have been tipped out of our aeroplane over France and should have landed in the place where there were quite a number of evil minded Bosch, whose one object would be to liquidate us before we could do the same to them. It all seemed so like an ordinary exercise, and this illusion (very fortunately) went on for one night up to the moment I landed with a bump in a field.

The doors of the aircraft were opened while we were still over the sea and being number one to jump in my aircraft I had a grand view as the coast of France appeared below us. I could see no sign of life below us, thanks to the R.A.F., and although I believe a few shots were fired at us I never saw any. I remember my signaller who jumped number two saying "Gawd! look at those bomb craters!" however we were soon over those, and fortunately I picked up a landmark and I knew we were coming in at more or less the right place. A few moments more and the red light came on and then the green and out I went, my mind a complete blank as usual when I jump. I can remember very little of my descent, it didn't take long anyway. I did rather a poor landing, my own fault entirely and bruised my knees which made crawling almost painful, and I had a certain amount to do during that day! Anyway I scrambled to my feet and unhitched myself from my parachute and took a look round. I knew I was more or less in the right place as others were coming down in the vicinity, but I was not exactly sure where. There was a horse grazing in the field where I was, who didn't seem to like my presence much, so I went off in the direction where I thought our rendezvous was. There were some machine guns firing at the planes over to the East and quite a lot of flak and stuff to the south but no sign of any enemy in our vicinity or in the direction I was going. There were numerous others from our battalion and in a little while I met one of my platoon commanders and then the Colonel and then another Captain and we checked our position and arrived at our objective, a quarry, without any untoward incident.

At this quarry was a cottage, and when we arrived, the French family came out and we shook hands all around and wished each other "Bon jour", most inappropriately! as it was then 2 am and the "jour" was not at all "bon". 2am "D-Day". The remainder of the battalion then began to arrive and so did one or two enemies. First a car whizzed down the road and got right through, we did throw a grenade at it, but it didn't stop it, but only bounced a rifle out of it, which I pinched as I only had a revolver. Then a motor cyclist buzzed through, he very nearly got through but was stopped a bit down the road.

After a bit we moved off, I hadn't got all my company by then by any means, but after about another hour I got the large majority. One or two of course never turned up including my company second in command, he, (I found later), had been killed soon after landing. He was a great loss as not only was he a very solid stand-by in times of stress, being an experienced soldier having fought in Tunisia and was quite imperturbable but he was also a very good friend of mine. He was rather a remarkable character, as he was well over forty, and had run away from home in the last war and joined up and since then had wandered all over the world, gold mining, engineering and cattle ranching besides having served as a merchant seaman in his spare time.

My company position was away from the rest of the battalion and during that morning we were left more or less in peace except for the odd sniper. One or two Frenchmen would keep coming and sitting at my headquarters and talking all about the evils of the Germans, they were rather a nuisance really as we were trying to keep hidden and they made no attempt to conceal themselves from the direction of the enemy and I rather felt they were quite likely to tell the Bosch where we were. I was rather glad when a bang went off in the neighbourhood, (one of our men blowing something up), and I was able to paint a lurid picture of an enemy attack and the man disappeared hurriedly . . .

By this time however the sea landing had been made, in fact some time before. The barrage put down on the coast was terrific and was just one continuous explosion and noise for some time, quite indescribable really, and most cheering to us. A few hours after the sea landing the commandos got up to us and came across our bridges, again most cheering, as things were a bit hectic just then. I remember that one lot had a piper with them, which was the first thing we heard of them, and a very pleasant sound it was, and I have taken a better view of bagpipes ever since! I remember thinking it was like the siege of Lucknow, I believe they heard bagpipes too didn't they? but we weren't in quite such a desperate state as they were. In fact as I said my company were being left alone at that time. This went on until about 5 p.m. when I was relieved on my side of the village by some troops of another battalion and I went down through the village

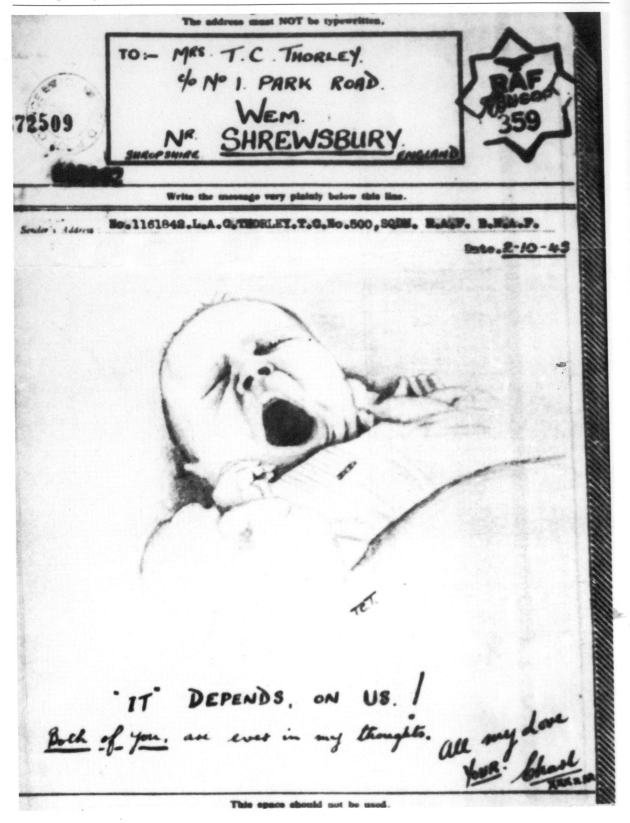

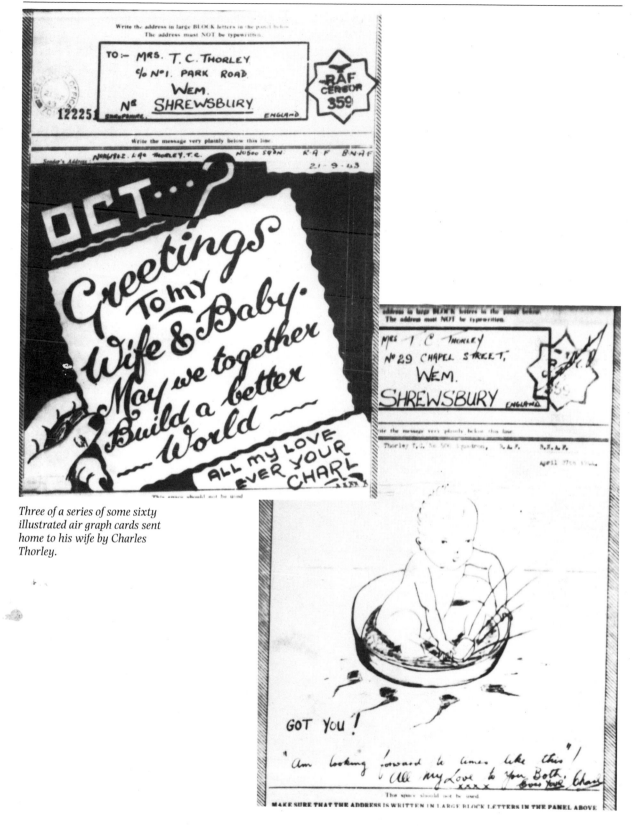

Three of a series of some sixty illustrated air graph cards sent home to his wife by Charles Thorley.

and took up a position in front of the battalion. I was rather widely scattered, having one platoon in a long hedgerow, about two or four hundred
yards to my right and the other two platoons and myself were round a
cross-roads, the trouble was the ground between my right platoon and
myself was quite open, and to reach it I had to go right back into the village
and up a track. There were some enemy about two hundred and fifty or
three hundred yards ahead of me beyond my cross-roads and I was told
to send one platoon to take the spot, but although we put guns and mortars
on to them, we found they were still quite bobbish and as they were in
crops about two feet high it was difficult to spot their exact position and
as soon as I started to move my platoon about five machine guns opened
up not only from the front but the sides as well so we gave up the idea
of taking the ridge, as it was a bit much for one platoon.

Nothing much happened for the remainder of the evening except the
odd sniper and machine fire, but about midnight just before a company
of another battalion was going to move forward on to the ridge where my
platoon was to have taken, the enemy started a hell of a hullabaloo first
at us and then at the hedgerow where my right hand platoon was, first
it was only machine guns, but when they switched to the hedgerow they
started putting up flares and coloured lights and they also had about six
self propelled guns, i.e. guns mounted in tanks, which were firing right
into the hedge. They went right up to the hedge at least it looked like it,
and they also had some infantry with them as you could hear them shouting. Anyway in about twenty minutes the tumult and the shouting died
and all was quiet again. I was a bit depressed during all this, as I thought
that my platoon there, had undoubtedly all been liquidated, and also I
thought that they would probably attack us next. However they didn't and
we heard the guns going away in the distance. When the company went
through onto the ridge they found no-one there, so looking back on it I
presume the noise and 'carry-on' was to cover the withdrawal of the troops
immediately in front of us, I wish I had thought of that at the time, as
we might have hastened their departure, or delayed it indefinitely! The
rest of the night was quite peaceful for us. There was a lot of bombing
going on of the enemy back areas and a bit of enemy bombing of the beach
head. The next morning there was quite a bit of mortar fire soon after it
got light and also an armoured car came whizzing down the road towards
our cross-roads but unfortunately saw our anti-tank mines and stopped
just before reaching them, and our anti-tank gun with us missed it completely. I was, for some extraordinary reason, standing by the hedge
between the guns and the armoured car, goggling at it and waiting for
it to run over the mine, and when the gun went off the shell went uncom-
fortably close to my left ear. The car then went off the road and away,
the gun took another shot at it this time whizzing past my right ear.

I expect you are wondering what had actually happened to the platoon
in the hedgerow so I will skip back a bit to its story. After things quietened
down in that area during the night, I sent a patrol to try and find out
who was holding the hedgerow. After a bit they returned and said they
had contacted the sentry of the platoon, and the impression I got was that
he seemed rather surprised that anyone should doubt their continued
existence! The next morning I found out from the officer there the account

of the party. It appeared that when the do started they moved along the hedge a bit and sat tight, neither firing nor moving. The tanks didn't come near enough for their anti-tank mortar and the infantry didn't either, and eventually they drifted off as we saw from the other side. Actually my journey over to this platoon was the cause of my downfall. As I said before there was quite a bit of mortar fire going on, mainly on the company who had gone through onto the ridge beyond us, but it was also coming down on other spots too, roads etc. anyway I went back to the outskirts of the village through an orchard and started to go up the track towards the hedgerow. This track was out in the open, and although it had a few bushes on it, there wasn't much cover. However, that didn't worry me at all as there didn't seem to be any enemy round about to matter much and there were only three of us, Porteus, one of my orderlies carrying a wireless and myself. We had got about half way up this track, we had to go about three hundred yards in all when a burst of mortar fire came down in the field about a hundred yards to our left. No one took any notice as it didn't do any harm I thought it was just a bad shot for the road or the orchard behind us. However, after about another two minutes another four bombs came down, this time astride the track and only about fifteen yards ahead of me. We all went flat on our faces, and as I was falling I felt something hit my arm, just as if a bit of earth or a stone had been thrown hard against it, it didn't hurt at all, and as I got up I looked at my sleeve and couldn't see a hole so I thought "that's OK I've got away with that", actually the hole was in the seam and had cut my whistle lanyard in half as clean as a knife. However, I hadn't time to notice that then as I noticed that Porteus was still on the ground and had been hurt. It seemed from what he said and where the wound appeared to be that he had been hit in the stomach which wasn't so good and we got him a bit under and got some stretcher bearers who came very quickly. I then went on with the battalion's second-in-command to my platoon. By this time, my arm was pretty stiff and I could feel it bleeding down my arm, so I knew I had been hit! I found my platoon OK and quite happy, so I went back to my company head-quarters and the medical orderlies tied my arm up. I wasn't feeling too good by now, a bit of shock I suppose, anyway I recovered a bit with the help of some whisky I had with me, and went into the village to the Battalion Aid Post via Battalion Headquarters and from there I was sent to the main dressing station in a chateau, where I learnt that I was being evacuated, they had just started evacuating people by then. I saw Porteus in the M.D.S.* looking none too good, and after that I heard nothing of him until I had a letter from him a few days ago. Until then I had no idea if he was alive or dead, and I thought the latter was more likely. Actually his wounds were not as bad as I thought and he had been hit in the chest and arm and not his stomach. I was taken from the M.D.S. to the beach ambulance where I remained about four hours. There was still the odd sniper about in the houses near the beach and marines kept bobbing about looking for them. The beach and the sea were an amazing sight, the whole sea was covered with ships of all kinds landing craft merchantmen and warships of all sizes some of whom were firing landwards.

*military dressing station

While we were there an enemy fighter came over, machine gunned the beach and about the only enemy fighter I had seen at all.

We were eventually embarked on a tank landing craft, via a "duck". It was rather amazing really, as we got into this "duck" (I expect you have seen pictures of them) which went down to the waters edge and went into the sea and out to the landing craft which had its ramp down, and the "duck" went up the ramp and unloaded us right inside the ship, incredible really. The voyage back was uneventful and monotonous. I was very hungry as I hadn't had a proper meal since leaving England, I found I didn't want to eat and had to make myself eat two pieces of chocolate and a biscuit, and Porteus had made tea for us twice when we had a spare moment. Anyway on the ship I felt I could eat a horse and I learned from a French commando that if I went to the galley I would find something so I did and found some tea and the cook gave me a tin of beefsteak and kidney pudding, I had never tried the tinned variety before and most excellent it was. I think one tin was supposed to be about enough for three anyway I ate the lot!

Well that seems to be about all. A lot of it I've given rather sketchily and I could never hope to give you the atmosphere, as it were, it is really quite indescribable. The extraordinary smell of broken bombed buildings and explosives; the countryside, very like the Cotswolds really, littered with gliders and parachutes; gliders everywhere, in hedges and fences, some broken so much that it looked that no-one could have survived and yet in very few cases was any one hurt on landing. It was really an amazing but very unpleasant and tragic two days. The second in command of my company never appeared at all and was found four days later he had been killed soon after landing; and my best friend in the battalion never turned up at all nor any one from his plane, so what happened to him I don't know. After I left they had rather a sticky time and most of the officers were either killed or wounded more the latter than the former fortunately. Our Colonel was killed, the announcement was in today's Telegraph (July 23rd). I am afraid I have taken about ten days to write this letter but I thought you might like to hear all about it. We are now staying with one of Elsbeth's aunts in a perfectly lovely little thatched cottage. Elizabethan but with all modern conveniences! . . .

Yours ever,
Gerald

———

Cedric Carryer served as a lieutenant with No. 44 Royal Marine Commando, which had sailed for the Far East in November 1943. At the time this letter was written, the Commando was in India, following operations in the Arakan and Assam.

'X' Troop
44 (R.M.) Commando,
India Command
29.6.44

My Darling Mummie,
Still no air letter cards, so I have had to fall back on this. I will warn you now, that I have really very little news at all, but I suppose I shall blather on somehow, and if you don't mind it, I really rather enjoy it. Still no sign of your lost letter; I suspect that some more are missing during that period. It is rather annoying using one of these, because I really don't know how long it will take to reach you, and you may receive an A.G. Card, before

you get this. It is rather pot luck, as they sometimes take two weeks, and sometimes three months – if it is the latter, I shall be very annoyed, as it costs me eight annas.

On Friday I had my first game of rugger, since I have been in this part of the world. I played for the Commando against a combined R.A.F. team, and we drew with no score. This was not very surprising, as the ground was very very wet, and the threequarters had no chance at all. On each touch line, there was a ditch containing about two feet of mud and water. When I was first tackled, I did a nice somersault into it to my great discomfirture, but also to the delight of the crowd. A little later on, I sent him for a bath instead, and whereas I went in posterior leading, he went in head first. The Marine laughs last!! Afterwards we had a bit of a party to celebrate two of our Officers promotion. There was plenty of booze for everyone, so I enjoyed myself (We must keep this malaria away you know!) Afterwards we went to a picture show, and saw Flanagan and Allen in "We'll Smile Again", which was a most amusing and refreshing show. We smiled again and again.

It is very difficult to write this letter, as the other four officers are having a terrific discussion. It started off with venereal disease, passed through pantomimes and post war problems, and has now reached schoolmasters.

We always find something to interest us in the evenings, whether we read, talk write or just play cards. Some people find life rather boring, but luckily I never do. Tomorrow evening we are going to have a Brains Trust, and I think it ought to be really rather amusing. The 'Trust' is more wit than brains, but that will probably make it all the better. Crosswords are still the vogue among the officers, and you can almost hear the wheels

A happy recipient of a letter from home.

going round at night. We have also got a buzzer, and spend a lot of time practicing morse; I can now send at 16 words a minute, and receive at ten. I'll make a Signals Officer yet. . . . .

Somehow I think you must have missed the newsreel about our operation, as several of the lads have had letters from their wives etc., who have seen it. One Sergeant was recognised in his home town, and immediately the cinema manager made some huge prints, and plastered his bearded countenance all over the town, and he became the hero of "Salute the Soldier" week!

One of the officers here is a very keen butterfly collector, and I have now become his chief assistant. We made a net out of bamboo and an unserviceable mosquito net, and we have already obtained some fine specimens. Someone shouts "Look, there's a monarch"; I don't know what a monarch is, but a huge winged creature brushed past my face. Cedric siezes net, and with eyes aglow, body bare and hair on end, pursues said elusive flutterby into the depths of the jungle. To the amazed onlookers there come faint words carried on a tiny breeze, distorted by jackals and crickets "missed 'im"!! However we get quite a lot of fun, and it passes the time away.

After breakfast this morning I was sitting on the bamboo pole, and considering life in general. Then I had one of my brilliant ideas, which often come to me at such moments. "O.K." you say "shoot, and get it off your chest" or words to that effect. I might add that this idea is copyright reserved, and anyone attempting to reproduce it will be crucified without full military honours, so beware, my little Barkbyites, you have been

Prisoners of war in the Far East were seldom allowed to write home. Very occasionally they were issued with pro forma post cards (right) or with cards on which they were limited to a set number of words (below). Thomas Smithson, a prisoner of war in Japanese hands, was suffering from malaria at a camp in Taiwan when he filled in the details on his card.

warned. At eight one evening, anyone who is not in bed, will see a B.B.C. recording car entering the damp unfriendly jungle. Some weeks later, at eight-O-clock, you are all sitting round your fire, listening to the wireless, when suddenly a voice says "This is for those who have relations and friends in the Burma Jungle; put out the light and be with them for a moment". So you put out the light, and suddenly the shrieks of the jackals, the noises of the birds, the crickets and the frogs break the silence. You hear the various idiosynchresies of our jungle companions, until your hair stands on end, and little girls say "Oh, Mum, your brother Berts out there, and 'e ain't frightened!" Not much he isn't! Then it stops and a voice says "You have been listening to 'Jungle Janglings, by kind permission of Cedrico Carriera, the Tiger Tamer"! Then Indian music and God Save the King. I think I must write to the B.B.C. about it, but I expect they are too busy in France. Just as if they have hyenas in Cherbourg!!

Being a marine out here, doesn't pay you very much, because we are

IMPERIAL JAPANESE ARMY
24.4.1943.

I am interned in Taiwan Prisoners' Camp, Nippon.

My health is excellent. usual. poor.

I am ill in hospital.

I am working for pay.

I am not working.

Please see that our future security is taken careof.

My love to you at Home
T. Smithson

SERVICE DES PRISONNIERS DE GUERRE
FROM:

Name   T. Smithson.
Nationality   British.
Rank   Private.
Camp TAIWAN PRISONERS CAMP. NIPPON.

PASSED
P.W. 6456

TO: SERVICE DES PRISONNIERS DE GUERRE
Mrs. T. Smithson,
3 Tomlin Square,
BOLTON,
Lancs.,
ENGLAND.

not only paid by the Admiralty instead of India Command, but also we have to pay home income tax. Hence an R.M. Commando Officer, in what are supposed to be crack troops, gets nine pounds less per month than an ordinary army lieutenant. It doesn't seem right somehow, and it annoys us very much. Also in India we get £150 a month colonial allowance, but the moment we come out here to fight, we only get 3/9d a day, because they say we are being provisioned. (The old corn dog jumps up and takes a bow). Of course these allowances are in addition to our normal rate of pay, but we were only informed a few days ago, and some of our nest eggs for leave arn't nest eggs any longer! Still we carry on, and the troops are wonderful, and waiting for another chance to knock Joe Jap for six.

10 P.M. Indian Standard time; 5.30 P.M. British double summer time. Here is the news and this is Whatshisname reading it. Very little has happened to the Jungle Boys. Lieut. Carryer has been awarded the N.B.C. for conspicuous gallantry in using a new SECRET weapon the Flit Spray against squadrons of small flies, most of which were brought down. 3 Flutterby 109s were caught in a trap, and may now be seen in Tent NO.4. It rained again and Cedric had a bath. That is the end of the news. Here is the weather forecast, "More Rain" Here is the Galley Front, The latest recipe for a Jungle Stew "Take one pint of water; if it is black, don't worry because it will be blacker still in a little while. Take three monsoon beatles and ground them up finely. Add some flies legs (these flies must be fully fledged and mature). Mix up with the hearts of a Preying Mantis, and the

Sorting mail in the Western Desert,
1942.

head of a tarantula. Now add corn beef indefinitely, and heat rapidly, and leave it to get cold by mistake. This dish will be found to be most delicious, if you close your eyes, hold your nose and think about 'Christmas'. Especially recommended for those who are unconscious. Yes, it gets you in the end; ever hear of Jungle Madness?

Well, I think I have just about told you all the news of importance. Remember that I miss you all a hell of a lot, and I often think about you and wonder what you are doing. I just can't thank you enough for all your letters, they are absolutely everything to me. Look after yourself, Mummie darling, and don't work too hard. Above all don't worry, as I am fine, and let's hope it won't be long before I am with you all again. My fondest love to everyone at home, and most of all for you, darling.

Ever and always your most loving son

Cedric

XXXX

———

Private Ivor Rowbery served with the 2nd Battalion, South Staffordshire Regiment attached to the 1st Airborne Division. This farewell letter to his mother was written in September 1944 before the Battle of Arnhem. The letter won first prize in the 1946 Basildon Bond Competition for the Best Letter Written by a Member of the Forces during the Second World War. It was published in the *Tatler & Bystander* on 18 September 1946. The magazine printed the following: 'This letter by a Wolverhampton working lad moves me more than some more celebrated literary efforts, and I am grateful to the boy's mother for her permission to reproduce it, "because it may help other parents".' The covering envelope was marked: 'To the Best Mother in the World.' Private Rowbery was killed at Arnhem on 17 September 1944.

Blighty

(Some time ago)

[undated]

Dear Mom,

Usually when I write a letter it is very much overdue, and I make every effort to get it away quickly. This letter, however, is different. It is a letter I hoped you would never receive, as it is just a verification of that terse, black-edged card which you received some time ago, and which has caused you so much grief. It is because of this grief that I wrote this letter, and by the time you have finished reading it I hope that it has done some good, and that I have not written it in vain. It is very difficult to write now of future things in the past tense, so I am returning to the present.

To-morrow we go into action. As yet we do not know exactly what our job will be, but no doubt it will be a dangerous one in which many lives will be lost – mine may be one of those lives.

Well, Mom, I am not afraid to die. I like this life, yes – for the past two years I have planned and dreamed and mapped out a perfect future for myself. I would have liked that future to materialize, but it is not what I will but what God wills, and if by sacrificing all this I leave the world slightly better than I found it I am perfectly willing to make that sacrifice. Don't get me wrong though, Mom, I am no flag-waving patriot, nor have I ever professed to be.

England's a great little country – the best there is – but I cannot honestly and sincerely say "that it is worth fighting for." Nor can I fancy myself in the role of a gallant crusader fighting for the liberation of Europe. It would be a nice thought but I would only be kidding myself. No, Mom, my little world is centred around you and includes Dad, everyone at home, and my friends at W'ton – *That* is worth fighting for – and if by doing so it strengthens your security and improves your lot in any way, then it is worth dying for too.

Now this is where I come to the point of this letter. As I have already stated, I am not afraid to die and am perfectly willing to do so, if, by my doing so, you benefit in any way whatsoever. If you do not then my sacrifice is all in vain. Have you benefited, Mom, or have you cried and worried yourself sick? I fear it is the latter. Don't you see, Mom, that it will do me no good, and that in addition you are undoing all the good work I have tried to do. Grief is hypocritical, useless and unfair, and does neither you nor me any good.

I want no flowers, no epitaph, no tears. All I want is for you to remember me and feel proud of me, then I shall rest in peace knowing that I have done a good job. Death is nothing final or lasting, if it were there would be no point in living; it is just a stage in everyone's life. To some it comes early, to others late, but it must come to everyone sometime, and surely there is no better way of dying.

Besides I have probably crammed more enjoyment into my 21 years than some manage to do in 80. My only regret is that I have not done as much for you as I would have liked to do. I loved you, Mom, you were the best Mother in the World, and what I failed to do in life I am trying to make up for in death, so please don't let me down, Mom, don't worry or fret, but smile, be proud and satisfied. I never had much money, but what little I have is all yours. Please don't be silly and sentimental about it, and don't try to spend it on me. Spend it on yourself or the kiddies, it will do some good that way. Remember that where I am I am quite O.K., and providing I know you are not grieving over me I shall be perfectly happy.

Well Mom, that is all, and I hope I have not written it all in vain.

Good-bye, and thanks for everything.

Your unworthy son,

IVOR

———

Ivor Rowbery.

George Leinster was a captain in the Sherwood Rangers Yeomanry, which had seen service in North Africa, before taking part in the Normandy campaign. This letter to his mother is a first-hand account of the British Liberation Army's advance through France, Belgium and Holland.

Capt. G. S. T. Leinster
Sherwood Rangers Yeomanry
B. L. A.
Friday 29th September 1944

My Dearest Mother,

If I am to write you the long letter I have been promising for several weeks, it must be typewritten, so please excuse that. I know you do not like letters so written. My failure to write earlier has not been due to being always on the move. Between our periods of movement and excitement we have been able to have short but very pleasant rests. These "rests" are often my busiest times, and somehow I always just failed to write the fuller type of letter. Often too, experiences crowded on one another so fast that there was too much to say in anything less than a small book. Now that another phase seems to have ended, it is possible to look back and see things in truer perspective.

I have told you of our joy to reach virtually undamaged towns and villages after being penned for so long in our narrow bridgehead, with its ruined villages and farms and dead cattle. We had one or two sharp brushes with Jerry before we broke through to do the 'hunting' which we still feel is our proper metier. The country from the Caen sector to the Seine is among the loveliest I have seen, but before we reached that we passed through an area of the dead which Dante could not have imagined in his wildest dreams.

This was the 'neck' of the Argentan-Falaise 'pocket' where our airforce and artillery wrought terrible slaughter among the retreating Germans. You will have read of this in the newspapers, but no description could do justice to the scenes which greeted us. It was grotesque and horrible, and we were all silent as we drove on beneath an incongruously bright sun; one felt that perpetual twilight should shroud such obscenity.

On that and on many other occasions we have felt that if the Germans were not such swines we could feel some pity for them. We feel not a shred of pity. I have talked with many German prisoners; I do not do so now as they make me feel so furious. They have a sort of mental leprosy which renders parts of their minds and emotions entirely insensitive. I know that when they were destroying and burning in their heyday they felt no pang or qualm for the suffering they caused. That they lack a sense of personal conscience is understandable, but it is baffling to find all their kinder emotions equally atrophied.

George Leinster.

How you who have not come into close contact with the Germans can hope to understand them I do not know. It is difficult enough for us who meet them constantly. I only hope that those who control our post-war relations with Germany shall be men who know the German as the Soldier does.

I could write for hours about Germans. I'll just say one thing more. Among the hundreds of thousands of prisoners we have taken are many who have had a damned good war. They have spent four years living on the fat of the land in France, Belgium and other occupied countries, with frequent home leaves during which they have been regarded as conquering heroes and little tin gods generally. Now after in many cases only a few days of real war they become prisoners for a few months – and then what? It seems to me to be all wrong for them to return home quietly. For them their war years will always be the best time of their lives and they will have seen little or nothing of the real face of war. I'd keep the whole lot of them as labourers for some years after the war under prisoner-of war conditions; and *no* home leaves. Mother, these men give one a terrible sense of futility; the war taught them absolutely nothing and they'll be delighted when they can start again. It is clear from their conversation that the suffering and destruction of war just do not register with them. Now that the war is taken to Germany itself perhaps a few will become converted to a more normal view; but it will be only a very few.

Of all the phony articles thrust upon the world, the notions of German culture and German honour must be given a high place. Their culture is veneer; their honour, self – or class – interest in a coloured wrapping. They are very good soldiers largely because they are taught to despise those individual and sentimental interests which make the average Englishman prefer civilian life to soldiering.

Already we have proof that while German officers may order their men to fight to the last, they must be careful not to sacrifice themselves, as they will be needed for Germany's next – and as they hope, final effort.

The Germans were very frightened of the Maquis, the armed civilians, in France and Belgium. It was the fear of a guilty conscience. They were delighted to surrender to us and so be protected against the vengeance of the partisans. Never was protection given less willingly. There were many cases in which natural justice was speedily meted out by the civilians. We could not countenance this when we were present, but did not regret it when we could not prevent it.

It is proverbial among the men that we always have our 'big days' on Sundays, and so it was that on Sunday 23rd of August the chase proper began. Instead of travelling on the tank I managed to make myself 'whipper in' for the column in a small armoured scout car. This allowed much freedom of movement and naturally I chose good strategic points, (such as town squares or roadside cafes) to make my halts so that I could check the column as it passed.

This was the real start of the 'liberation' march. The inhabitants of the

The people of Brussels welcome British troops, the day after the liberation of the city, 4 September, 1944.

burned and blackened strip of Normandy which had seen such bitter battles could not be expected to go frantic with joy after the first few days. These new villages and towns we passed through were quite different. For anxious weeks the people had known of the great battles being fought between themselves and the coast, and while they hated the Germans, they liked their families and homes to be in one piece. Their delight to see us charging through, tank after tank, for hours on end, without any fighting or damage, was overwhelming. Even the unfortunate ones who had suffered loss from the odd bomb or shell gave us a royal welcome.

The fruit was ripening in that lovely countryside, and from that day onwards we have eaten a huge quantity of apples, pears, plums and peaches. For mile after mile we drove through cheering crowds amidst a hail of fruit and flowers. Immediately a halt was made, each village was mobbed by people of all ages, and wines and liqueurs hidden from the Germans were thrust upon the crews. Throughout that day and many others we travelled far faster than the tank text-books contemplate and the mileage figures were surprisingly high.

I have described the first day at length, but the description holds for all our 'travelling' days since then. The joy of these folk must be seen to be believed. All say they knew we would come back some day but what a long time we have been! The British Tommy, as ever, is our best ambassador, and with his usual skill sweeps aside difficulties with the various languages.

The joy of the people is equalled only by their hatred of the Germans. This can almost be felt. Their great fear is that the mass of the English, so far away in detatched England, will again be too lenient towards the Germans owing to a mistaken sense of fair play. Most of them wish to see the Germans literally exterminated, and all say we must go right to Berlin and impose our will from there. We realise how fortunate we are that England is an island; it is hard for Englishmen to appreciate the feelings of these smaller countries who are on Germany's doorstep and who cannot stand up to Germany without strong support. I think our prestige has been very high since Autumn 1940, when we stood alone, but never in all our history has it been so high, at least in Europe, as it is today. This offers unprecedented opportunities for the future and it is in our hands whether we take them. I think the only way – but at least a possible way – we can bungle things is if we relapse into the pre-war apathy which permitted privilege, birth and money to persue their own ends without check.

It is quite embarrassing to be an Englishman in these countries. Incidentally, one is not an Englishman to these people; one is a Tommy, pronounced 'Tow-mee'. The French and Belgian children would sometimes ask us 'Are you American?' we would say 'No we are English', then with a look of great hero-worship they would say 'Tow-mee!' and run off to bring their parents to see a real Towmee.

All this adoration has acted like a tonic, and has brought out the best in us. When even the humblest soldier, whatever his job, is put on a pedestal because he is English, he does his best to live up to it. Relations between ourselves and the civilians have been rather better than excellent. To the young children, the Towmee is a legendary figure of whom their mothers have talked for years as a sort of St. George who would come one day to chase the wicked Germans away. When they really see us, it is rather like a child seeing Father Christmas in the flesh.

To the elder French and Belgians who remembered the last war, our arrival was no less welcome. They know the Tommy is anything but a legendary figure and is not lacking in faults, but they have had two wars of German occupation and to them our troops were very real liberators. Many were overcome with emotion. Their loathing for the Germans, these people who perhaps know them better than any others, was almost frightening . . .

The patriotism of the poor in all countries is remarkable; perhaps they seek to compensate in the spirit for what they lack in the material. We had few opportunities to enjoy the hospitality they offered, but on occasion a half-hour halt would permit a hurried sharing of a workman's meal and a glass of the inevitable wine. I suspect that the meat we ate had often been between a pair of shafts, but it was not too bad, and they were so happy to have us as passing guests.

Our journey was not wholly a peace-time sort of Lord Mayor's show. Periodically we met enemy rear-guards who would take their toll before being eliminated. Sometimes, but happily not often, it was necessary for us to destroy houses in which Germans were sheltering. Even in these cases, the inhabitants still greeted us regally. One small town was very badly damaged, but no sooner had the enemy been dealt with than the citizens came out from their holes and cellars with the customary fruits and drinks for us. There will be exceptions, but in general the spirit matters far more to the French and Belgians than material things; and their spirits had been sorely bruised for four long years.

It was strange to pass through all those towns so well-known in the last war. We were close to Armentieres, Vichy, Le Cateau, Mons, and passed through Amiens and Arras, both taken almost without a fight. It was strangest of all to see the hugh cemeteries of the last war, stretching away over the plains with their limitless rows of small white crosses, the imagination boggling over so much slaughter. None of this war's cemeteries, not even that at Alamein, compare in size with these we saw, and I still think that this is an easy war for the soldier in every way in comparison with that of 1914-1918. My driver's father – and many another man's father too – was buried in one of the cemeteries; I think he felt as I did that we were doing our best to atone for our breach of faith in the inter-war years. I believe the older Frenchmen and Belgians feel the same. Can you imagine these men's feelings in 1940? They had managed to survive one terrible war which had devastated their country, they had lived through the following years of want and trouble and disillusion, and then after another brief but painful war it seemed that all their life of struggle and sacrifice had been in vain. How happy is England never to have been invaded. When I read the speeches of some of our head-in-the-cloud or head-in-the-sand dignitaries in England regarding European affairs, men who have never wanted for anything their whole lives through and who cannot understand why everyone does not go to a public school and dine at the Berkely, I become speechless.

The Belgians we liked immensely. Although the frontier was merely a wire fence across the fields, we noticed changes immediately. They are very clean and well turned-out, even the poorest, and take great pride in their homes. I was surprised to find them so different from the French in many ways – quite wrongly, I had always thought of them as Frenchmen's small brothers. They have a distinctive Belgian culture, and perhaps because they are so small and defenceless, are very Belgian. We were treated with great hospitality in spite of the great shortage of many necessities. I was able to more or less live in a railwayman's house for three days during a halt. The family could not have been kinder. What beasts the Germans are to bring war twice within a generation to such good people.

Our welcome in Belgium was a little more restrained than in France, but certainly no less sincere. Whenever we stopped for the night – and *if* we stopped for the night – our area immediately looked like the Town Moor during Race Week. The entire population would settle around us and show wondering interest in our cooking and sleeping arrangements. Everyone made friends with everyone else, and if operations permitted, those men who were free would soon be the centre of attraction in a home or restaurant. It was always a little worrying for me when fresh orders came to move on, but the men behaved well, and with a little help from civilians would manage to be on their tanks in time. Great fun.

We had felt a little doubtful about the Dutch, but our doubts were soon proved ill-founded, and again we had the now familiar sight of crowded, cheering streets. I'm afraid Holland will show some scars before the last Germans leave it, but the Dutch are a proud, independent race who are more than willing to pay that price. We like those we have met very much indeed.

Near where we are living at the moment is a most charming woman,

Soldiers of the Fifth Army writing home from Italy, November, 1943.

a surgeon's widow, with her small children. She has left one of the towns where there is fighting and has taken possession of a beautifully furnished house owned by a wealthy bachelor friend. He went "underground" some weeks ago on learning that the Gestapo wanted him, and no-one knows his whereabouts. He does not know his house is being used. This lady lights huge log fires for us in the evening, and we have a nightly conference there. We have crates of captured wines, liqueurs and spirits, and these nightly conferences are highly enjoyable after the rather cold and wet days out in the open. We *do* sometimes wonder what the owner would say if he walked in one night to find a dozen or so English officers reclining in his best chairs, but our hostess assures us he would be delighted, as he only lives for Holland.

This woman is well-read and widely travelled, she's very attractive too. I have long talks with her; a nice change from the tank crew!

I must tell you something about the Maquis, the armed civilians in all these countries. They have been invaluable to us in taking and looking after prisoners until our infantry could catch us up. With tens of thousands of Germans retreating in small parties with only the haziest idea of what was happening, these patriots have had the time of their lives. It is really a terrible thing when a modern army loses cohesion; for several weeks Jerry just didn't have the vaguest idea of what was happening anywhere. His Normandy armies lost all their heavy equipment and disintegrated into groups with either out-of-date orders or no orders at all. These were easy meat for the Maquis.

In Belgium particularly we worked closely with the civilians, and during one period took, with them, several thousands of prisoners, these were a real embarrassment to both ourselves and the Maquis until we could hand them over. Even Germans get hungry sometimes. It was perfect poetic justice that the German garrison troops who had lorded it for so long over the civilians should be taken often without any struggle by those same civilians and locked in the village school or church hall.

I had one amazing night in Belgium. Three Maquis chaps who had been co-operating with us suggested jokingly that we should go to Brussels. They had a high-powered German car, and the distance was about 60 miles. There was doubt however as to whether the roads to Brussels from where we were was clear of Germans, though we had heard that Brussels had been entered by some of our troops. The Colonel very sportingly gave us his blessing, so with one other officer and the three Maquis, off we went. Two of the Maquis travelled on the mudguards with their sub-machine guns at the ready. We travelled very fast and I expected them to be thrown off any moment, even if the cold did not make them loosen their holds and fall. These fellows wore mostly civilian clothes but had picked up odds and ends of German, Belgian and British military equipment, and clothing. They looked just like bandits or Chicago gangsters.

We arrived safely in Brussels, and still carrying their machine guns (Jerry was quick to shoot any of those men he captured) the patriots took us to a cafe-dansant place. Everyone in Brussels had gone completely haywire, and there we were seized, hugged, danced with, dragged around, kissed, buffeted, cheered, and generally worn down. The Maquis boys kept their machine guns with them until the locals finally persuaded them there were no Germans left in the city, and then we all hid our arms behind the bar. We finished with hordes of visiting cards from people who wanted us to call upon them or stay with them when we had the chance. Everyone of all ages was quite loopy that evening, but their joy was entirely sincere. We expected to see Brussels again but were moved too soon.

From the restaurant we were taken to some of the small bars where for years the Resistance movement had held secret meetings. When the full story can be told, the World will be astonished to learn the strength of these underground movements and the diverse ways in which the British gave them constant aid, even when we were very weak ourselves. But if any German comes up to me and tells me has always been a member of a Resistance movement in Germany . . .!

We had a speedy return to a town near where the regiment was stationed. Here we were taken to the headquarters of the local Maquis. We found the leader very worried, and very relieved to see us. It appeared they had nearly 1000 Germans locked in the town schools and had had them there for 2/3 days. They had been able to take all these prisoners in small parties while they were passing through the district trying to get back to Germany; most of them had surrendered without much trouble on being told that English tanks were all around them. (The Germans had by this time begun to panic at the mention of English tanks). Now, however, after 2/3 days, the Germans were beginning to think they had been hood-winked by the Maquis as they had seen no sign of English troops, and were working themselves up into an ugly mood. My arrival at Maquis H.Q. at 4 a.m. must have seemed like an Act of Providence to their leader, though personally I was beginning to feel that bed was the best place in Belgium, as in the Middle East. The Maquis had very few arms among them, and I could not refuse their request, so off I went round all the school buildings to show my face and uniform. I think the Jerries were very pleased to see me indeed; conscience doth make cowards of us all. In that place they had shot 5 wounded maquis after taking them prisoner, and feeling in the town was running high. I told them they would be taken to official prisoner of war camps as soon as we could spare some transport to take them there. (This annoyed some of the Maquis who thought the Jerries should have been marched to the French coast; or wherever they were going. Quite apart from any other consideration that is too long a job). I also told them, a little peevishly that if Germans *would* surrender by hundreds of thousands, they must expect to wait a little before being transported to our lines. Fortunately I was able to arrange for lorries to call a few hours later to take all the Germans away. Sometimes we had to protect German prisoners from the populace.

Our long chase ended with a very dirty little battle on one of the canals. Bridgeheads are strange things; once you're over, you just dig your teeth in and resolve to stay there. We thought it would be that way on "D" day, but actually it was much easier. In this instance we just went bowling along with no idea that Jerry would at least try to push us back, and suddenly there we were right in the middle of quite a warm area. We kept our teeth in, and it was Jerry who went back, but it was a bitter fight. I lost a very fine friend there, and more old faces were missing when we moved on again. Men could not die in a better cause, but in the quiet of

Officers censoring mail in Italy, 1944.

Examples of the censor's handiwork.

Dear Mum & Dad,

I expect I'm

worried as you have not ~~...~~
~~...~~ time. It was a case of jetting
night and doing a moon light flit. ~~...~~
time that we embarked we had to ~~...~~
again as the sea was supposed to be too
rough. The next day we went across okay and
marvellous to relate I wasn't seasick not even
when we were in the middle of ▮▮▮▮▮▮▮▮
which surprised me. I reckon there must be
an old sea dog somewhere in the family. I
can tell you that we went through France
and I must say that we have been very well

EXAMINED
BY
BASE CENSOR

A. F. W. 3312

the night when the excitement dies, one grieves for their families. It must be done, and we are proud to be to the fore . . .

Anecdotes about the "chase" are legion. One which made me laugh a lot was the story of our reconnaissance troop which cautiously entered a village to see whether Jerry had left it. They suddenly noticed that the hands on the Church clock were going round and round at great speed. Suspecting that this was some enemy signalling arrangement, they elevated their guns and fired the machine-gun at the clock-face. A few minutes later a very shaken Belgian curate stumbled out of the church and explained that his clock had stopped many weeks before, and now that the Germans had gone he thought he would repair it. Fortunately he was not hurt.

This is a very jumbled letter I fear. Even now the events of recent weeks are still too fresh for me to see them in sequence and perspective, but perhaps I have been able to give you some idea of how we have spent them.

Mail is arriving faster than ever from home just now. We have been receiving English papers the day after they are published, and have plenty to read though not much time to do it in. The cigarettes and tobacco were very welcome. If you are sending any more, please make it cigarettes only, as my tobacco stock is high just now. We left the Normandy area with piles of cigarettes, chocolate and sweets, but over some hundreds of miles these have been given away and given away until now we can only give away some of our issue cigarettes and chocolate. I wish we could have given away a hundred times as much. All these people had only a few rationed, foul cigarettes and had not seen chocolate for more than 4 years. How pleased they are when we give them a bar! They give us all they can, we give them all we can, there is no mention of money at all, and it is all quite a Christian affair. For 4 months now, money has just not meant a thing to me; I rather like it.

I must close. Take care of yourself – I should be back in a few months to tell you all the stories.

My love, Dear Mother, as Ever to All.

XXX   GEORGE   XXX

———

Edward Hill-Heathcock served as a bombardier in the Western Desert and in Italy with the 15th Field Regiment, Royal Artillery. This letter to Derek Watkins, a neighbour back in England, was written from Italy.

November 10th. 1944

14585281 a/Bdr Heathcock EH.
RHQ 15th Field Regt. RA CMF.

Dear Derek,

I am afraid I have been neglecting all my old pals of late, and really that is a thing I want to do least of all. Here men come and go. Mainly "mucking in" and generally pretty decent. But always at the back is the same self-preservation instinct, so that come danger, they would willingly help each other to escape. And today, all over the world, the old mates from Shanty Town are slogging away in filth and wet and disease, and every now and then, as you at home probably know sooner than I, one drops out of the running and there is another gap in that young band of kids who grew up together and disappear in such out of the way places, missed? perhaps, by those on the spot. Generally just "another guy" to them.

So I guess I just feel like writing a bit, to you in 57, who most of all

I know where you are, and hoping you are not too old yet. Probably you know most of my wanderings since I left you, the contrasting independence of overseas Army life for a kid of 19, and the almost childish way the laws govern even your dress, your daily habits. I won't say it hasn't been interesting, it has, providing one can wear a hard suit of semi-callousness and refuse to take anything to heart.

I enjoyed the desert, the vast timeless solitudes of it all, the ageless quality that makes 70 years seem such a *drop* in the ocean of time. The cities though, have all been well, just cities. Perhaps on account of their man made similarity, the similarity of the amusements – the fashions – of the lot I probably enjoyed Rans most this last time. And that I think because for the first time I had really been up against it all, up against the knowledge that tomorrow might not be, and getting a definite shape out of the old rut of endless tomorrows and a belief in yourself that you would always be around to see the next New Year in kinda thing. Well, it's a feeling you can never quite get used to.

So you see old man, it's a pleasure to write to a bloke who is still as I knew him – (I hope!) and who I very definitely hope is not worried about catching the old "Sunbeam special" in a morning when I am "polishing up the harness on a Friday night!" or its equivalent. Thinking about, I'd sooner have you on the floor with your blankets here than either of the blokes I HAVE got, but when I light home full of back pay and memories, I shall be even gladder to find you THERE. Geoff has been on his back for 18 months in India. Ralph, after 2 years silence, has sprung up in this

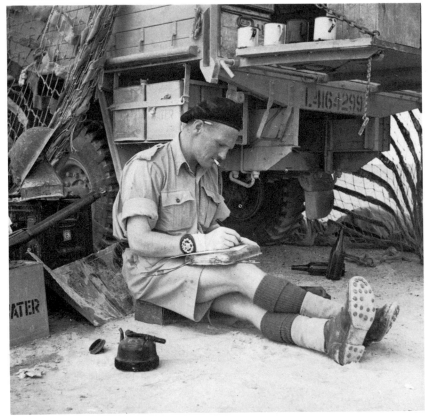

A quartermaster sergeant finds a quiet moment, Western Desert, 1942.

country with a letter. Chas has warned Jean and I guess they won't see *anybody* for another 5. Cousins I have I know not where exactly, Tony Rewherry somewhere in Egypt now, Graeme Weanly 'unknown destination' Bert Foley with the Japs, we hope. Blimey what a world.

As it is, this should just arrive around an'about Xmas. A lovely bleak one for all of us, thoughts and memories of the gay, tinsel ones, when half the fun was the coloured tape round the parcels. Always we seem to say "Next Year-next year" an echo down the Years an' years that dims the previous ones when it WAS a Christmas of lights and care-free laughter and pine trees. Sometimes one wonders whether *these* are the real ones, and those others just sweet pipe dreams, gone with the cold dawn, and perhaps you will *always* spend them pitching on a boat in the Atlantic, nursing the guns and waiting for the black crosses from the sky, or staring into the darkness with cold steel beads glistening with frost in the moonlight, soft strains of an infinitely sad gramaphone streaming with the golden lamp light through a glassless blankeyed window. (perhaps, somewhere there ARE cities of men, with real glass still in the frames, and soft beds and cushions and always warmth and dryness inside, with the carpets and chairs and radios. To you, a radio is an oblong box that generally gets damned awkward just as you want to save your own skin through it. Is it *always* going to be empty shells, four walls and sweeping the broken glass away to lie on the floor in your blankets? Perhaps it is I dunno Perhaps one country in the continent of Europe and Asia still retains wholeness and sanity, and all its men are scattered in snows and holes throughout the rest of it. But its still there, thank Heaven this Christmas and the women are still dressed decently and living like humans should in 1944.

So perhaps again, you don't mind that this desolation is Italy, or that ruin was Cassino or Caen or Cologne. Because Brum is still there, and the 2.10 still runs from Paddington, and Clent Hills have no slit trenches among the hedges and shell marks marring the gorse. *Unfortunately the white crosses are* in Italy too.

Still you may be sure I am thinking of you this time next month old man, hoping you are fit and well, and steaming ahead with the work and your hobbies and amusements, my best regards to your mother, who will probably ask why the dickens I came in at the 'front' when I arrive – and to your father, whose lettering always made me jealous when it came on a Christmas card envelope. And perhaps Catherine and David John will be seeing Stan soon, unless he has yet to cover the 21 mile anti-tank ditch to arrive home. From memory I don't think he should be over bothered, – after all, what's a Bailey Bridge more or less these days! (That bloke should be the toast of the 8th this winter, because without him it would still be south of Rome)

And to yourself, good wishes. No presents, no decent cards, but the thought old man, is there, – perhaps stronger than ever because of their absence.

And good luck,

Ever yours

Teddy

This letter was written by a South African padre to the mother of Gilbert Morgan, a soldier serving with the King's Shropshire Light Infantry, who was convalescent.

From A.P. Reesberg
312010(V) U D F
93 Brit. Gen. Hosp.
C M F

22/10/44

Dear Mrs. Stokes,*

It is with much pleasure and delight that I take up pen to write you a few lines. I met your son here in C.M.F. and he gave me permission to write. Also requesting you to keep my home address until such time as he returns safely to you and home. Your son is well and naturally would like to see this war to the end and do his little effort. It cannot be very long now, God willing I can safely predict 1945 A.D. as the finish of it all including Japan. And then – everybody home to a renewed life. We are becoming wiser daily, love our mothers more and more. But it cannot help us if we know our dear Mothers are worried about us. We like you to think and pray for us, but trust in God to see us safely through and in him rest safely by night. It will not help us to worry overmuch. Does God not say he loves the young and the old. And do we not see what babes we were when in the twenties, when we came to three score years. Rest assured dear Madam, that as God loves you who are grey, so he loves and cares for your son who is young. Again I say your son is quite well and his *chief illness today* is only that you might be worried and thereby become ill, and that when he comes marching home, *you might not be well enough to see him and be proud of the way he is stepping out.* I'll have to conclude slowly for I do not wish to bore you by making this letter too long. Again I will say to you do not forget *Grace*, *Mercy*, and *Peace*. And in these *three* your son asks you not to worry, he'll be home safely before the end of 1945, perhaps sooner. Let me call myself a friend of the family, will you? Thank you! And as such,

Yours Sincerely,
A. P. Reesberg

P.S. By the way I am an old married man, with a nice wife and two sons. A mother of your age, and a mother-in-law the same.

*Gilbert Morgan's mother had remarried.

Gilbert Morgan.

Leading Aircraftman Sam
Carson served as a medical
orderly with the Royal Air Force
in Iraq and Egypt.

1105717 LAC CARSON.S.
S.S.Q – R.A.F. FAT
M.E.FORCES.
Sat. 30th Dec.1944

Hello Folks,

Stand by for the greatest *SENSATION* of all times – Yes folks, it has happened at last *I AM COMING HOME!!*

Boy, you can talk about feeling in high spirits – today I feel right on the top of the world and why not, for this is to me, and I am sure it will be to you, *The greatest news since "D" Day*, I only received the glad news one hour ago so I thought I would sit down and write you straight away.

Although I am 7 weeks overdue folks, the news came as a bit of a surprise to me for all the Medical Orderlies up till now have been running up to 3 months overdue before getting home.

What do you think of this folks? just *one hour* before I received the great news, I received three letters from Home, one contained the letter you sent on from Bert Moreland – the other 2 were Xmas cards, one from "all at Monksbridge" and one from Henry & Cathie – in the one from Monksbridge the last two lines on the Xmas Card are *"Tis our sincere and constant Prayer You'll soon come home from over there"* and the last two lines on the one from Harry & Co. are *"May fortune smile on you today – And send word soon you're on your way"* Well folks, fortune certainly *HAS* smiled on me today – *so get the band out folks, kill the fatted calf, – "Gee, how the old town has changed"* I can hear myself say it now.

I still cant give you the exact date to expect me folks, but don't write anymore, for I expect to leave this station a week tomorrow Jan 6th. From here I go to a clearing off station, but just how long I will be there I can't really say – If I say I shall be home either the last week in January or the first week in Feburary I dont think I will be far out, however I will write again soon and give you the "Gen".

So-long Folks – "I'll be seeing you"

Love to all from Sam.

XXX for the wee ones!

———

Major Peter Gadsdon served as a
company commander with the
4th Battalion, 14th Punjab
Regiment, during the Burma
campaign. In 1945 he received
the Military Cross for his
leadership in the action at Letse,
which he describes in this letter.

21.3.45

Dear Mum and Dad,

I wrote to you a few days ago, but a couple of our outgoing mails have got lost, so I start again.

I remember saying that our war had become a mite static.

Foolish thought that the Japs would allow it to be so! He kept things nice and warm by bringing up some guns and proceeding to attack our dump and supplies, back in the rear, the night before last.

So yesterday morning bright and early found me setting off once more to restore the situation in the box, (you remember we marched on the same errand in the Arakon a little over a year ago). As we got near it it became apparent that there was quite a battle in progress, mostly our stuff firing, so I crossed my fingers and in we went.

Arrived inside the wire we found the war was on in the far corner. I was trotted off to see the Brigadier by a character who had to come and saluted me smartly in the middle of the track, with the result that I was sniped twice by a Jap up on the hill above! Good shooting too! As near as I have stood to one since Kohima days.

It turned out that we'd given the Jap a devil of a knock (there were fortynine draped on the wire in front of us), but there was still a number who had not been able to get away pinned down in holes in the ground all over the front at ranges of anything from forty to four hundred yards. Every time one moved he was shot at, and a number were blowing themselves up with grenades.

My orders in short were to go and get them, and then clear the whole area and chase the enemy. So off we went splitting my small force in half to do a neat pincers, I myself going with the left arm. I was moving with the foremost section about two hundred yards outside the wire when I noticed movement under a bush, so throwing up my rifle I took a snapshot and scored a miss! I then closed a ring round the character and to my delight found an officer badly wounded but alive! He was made prisoner and sent back where I believe he gave information before he died. One more sword in our collection!

We then worked through the village ahead killing about ten. They just fight to the last – typical example of one wounded – my chaps put a round over his head and shout "hands up!" He puts his hands up. We start to close in on him. He goes for a grenade we all dash for cover! Then we start again, until he throws the grenade whereupon my chaps fill him up with lead. They just have no sense. We only got the officer because he was past reaching for a grenade.

Arrived at the far end of the village I see the right arm of my pincer swinging in towards me, when suddenly the wire starts on my left. News

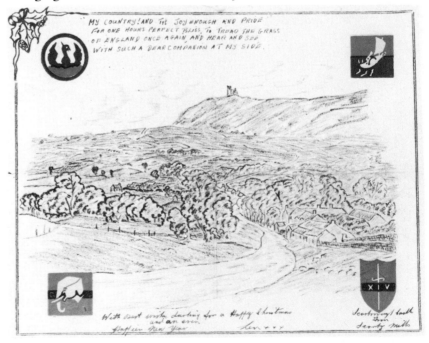

This Christmas card was drawn on an air mail letter card by Leonard Hughes, while he was serving with the Fourteenth Army in Burma, and sent to his wife.

is of ten Japs, and one of my men wounded and lying out in the open. Off I go at the double, get the rest of my outfit, and working round the enemy flank, put in a charge. Ten Japs! Hells bells, we were in a hornets' nest of nearly a hundred! Up starts a machine gun, over go a couple of my chaps, and there we are with our faces in the dust, and a long crawl out assisted by the machine gun crackling overhead!

Once back I sent for help from the guns while we kept the Jap from running away. Rather close quarters and the Jap hand grenade being rather lighter than our's, he can throw it farther, and was pitching them in amongst us.

We plastered them with artillery and roared in again to find one machine gun still firing. It was at this juncture that I bagged one myself – a standing shot at a Jap in a trench at about seventy-five yards got him straight through the head.

They had by then had enough and with their usual disregard for the conventions, came out and charged us! Not once. But twice! Just what we had been waiting for. We laid out sixteen in neat rows.

That fixed it – about forty got up and ran like blazes straight into the people I had put to catch 'em. They killed ten.

After that the war died down and I was able to collect my wounded, although there were still some Japs about the area.

Altogether a good day's rabbit shooting, as we were able to claim that we had put paid to fifty Japs.

My chaps were very good, as always, and quite undeterred by the few casualties we suffered.

We are all hopeful that we have taught the Jap a lesson over which he will ponder for a few days. I don't know what the final count is up there but we have put a fair size force out of action. I am fit, but it gets damn hot to play these games now.

Love,
Peter

————

4th September, 1945

Gunner Bob Grafton was a prisoner of war in the Far East from 1942 to 1945. He had been captured on the fall of Singapore and sent to Burma, where he was forced to work on the construction of the Burma-Siam railway. This letter to his teenage sweetheart, Dorothy, was written soon after he was liberated. Dorothy and Bob were married in December 1945.

My dear Dorothy,

This is my first letter as a free man. I am devoting it to you darling as I know how much our thoughts are the same at this moment. With this letter starts a new life for both of us. Here too start the realisation of the dreams which for me, seemed too far away to ever come true. Yet, although our first weeks of freedom have been very quiet and uneventful because we have not fully realised that we *are free* we are as patient as ever.

Before I say much about us darling and believe me I have much to say, I want to explain the position about mail and news from Mum and Dad who I do hope are OK. During the three and a half years I received about five cards from Mum and Dad and about thirty letters and cards from you dear, all of these have been twentyfive words except one which was the only one dated before September, 1943. The first mail I received was in August, 1944 when I came down from Burma since being freed I have received seven cards dated between November, 1944 and June, 1945 all

Prisoners of war from the Far East being welcomed on their return home.

your's sweetheart. So you see darling I am anxious about all of your news being so scarce. Most of the letters I have to use for cigarette paper, it being scarce. I received a sweet little polyphoto of you dear which I framed and will bring home. The climate of the jungle is not as kind to you as I shall always be. I'm longing for a chance to write a very long letter to you before I receive your's and of receiving one of the Plymouth kind from you. This one is restricted to this sheet but believe me darling I cannot write to you quickly enough. Seeing that I escaped from Singapore and was captured in Padang Sumatra March 7th 1942 I wondered whether you had any false alarms about my being killed.

One thing I must say that if it were not for my Father and Mother's careful upbringing as a child I am sure I would be where so many others went under the tough conditions. But sweetheart, thankfully I believe I'm much fitter, stronger and more of a man for the experience than when I kissed you goodbye on the station in August, 1941. The next kiss will be the first since so watch out darling! I dreamed of you many, many times and such places, but the dreams always ended in my having to return to the hell on earth. It wont be like that. Let me know what dear old Len is doing at first opportunity and also photos darling. I still have tons to say and so little space every word is precious . . . Disappointing only room to say it briefly when I want to so much I love you, I love you, I think that you are the most courageous having waited so long.

Goodnight darling.

Tons of love and kisses.

Bob

Credits

I would like to thank the following authors and heirs for permission to publish previously unpublished letters, documents and photographs. I am also grateful to those who have given me permission to publish material already in copyright.

FIRST WORLD WAR

Extract from an essay by G. K. Chesterton.
Reprinted by permission of Miss D. E. Collins.

Poem 'In The Pink' by Siegfried Sassoon, 10 February 1916.
Reprinted by permission of Mr. George Sassoon.

Letter from Henry Gibson *to* his parents who lived in Morley, Yorkshire.
Lent by Mr. Bryce Reid (nephew).
Published: First published in this anthology.

Letter from an officer *to* Mrs. John Redford who lived in Shrewsbury.
Lent by Mr. William Osman (son-in-law of Mrs. Redford).
Published: First published in this anthology.

Letter from R. A. Scott Macfie *to* his father who lived in Chester.
Lent by Dr. Henry O. Paton (nephew).
Published: First published in this anthology.
Photograph of R. A. Scott Macfie kindly loaned by Dr. Henry O. Paton.

Letter from Arthur Preston White *to* his sister.
Lent by the Governors of Highgate School.
Published: First published in this anthology.

Letter from James Crawford *to* his employer in Banff.
Lent by Miss Winifred Crawford (daughter).
Published: First published in the *Banffshire Journal*, 1915.

Letter from Norman Burge *to* his mother who lived in Southsea, Hampshire.
Lent by Colonel P. B. I. O. Burge, M.C. (son).
Published: First published in this anthology.

Letter from Norman Down *to* his fiancée.
Reprinted by permission of the Bodley Head Ltd.
Published: First published in *Temporary Heroes* by Cecil Sommers, 1916.

Letter from Cyril Rawlins *to* his father who lived in Rugeley, Staffordshire.
Lent by Mrs. Vivienne Rawlins (widow).
Published: First published in this anthology.
Photograph of Cyril Rawlins kindly loaned by Mrs. Vivienne Rawlins.

Letters from Arthur De Salis Hadow *to* his wife who lived in South Kensington, London.
Lent by Mr. J. W. Jervois (grandson).
Published: First published in this anthology.

Letter from Reuben Elliott *to* his parents who lived in Camberwell, South London.
Lent by Mrs. D. A. Thompson (daughter).
Published: First published in this anthology.

Letter from Alfred Bland *to* his wife who lived in South London.
Lent by Mr. Richard Bland (grandson).
Published: First published in this anthology.
Photograph of Alfred Bland kindly loaned by Mr. Richard Bland.

Letter from Joseph Quinn *to* his sister who lived in Waterloo, Merseyside.
Lent by Mrs. Eileen Quinn (sister-in-law).
Published: First published in this anthology.
Photograph of Joseph Quinn kindly loaned by Mrs. Eileen Quinn.

Letter from John Staniforth *to* his parents who lived in Hinderwell, Yorkshire.
Lent by The Reverend John Staniforth.
Published: First published in this anthology.

Letter from George Noel Cracknell *to* his mother.
Lent by Mrs. Sally Woodrow (niece).
Published: First published in this anthology.

Letter from Eric Rupert Heaton *to* his parents who lived in Scunthorpe, Lincolnshire.
Lent by Miss I. M. Heaton (sister).
Published: First published in this anthology.

Letter from Daniel Sweeney *to* Ivy Williams who lived in Walthamstow, Essex.
Lent by Mrs. D. J. Finch and Mrs. L. Tomlinson (daughters).
Published: First published in full in this anthology Extracts appeared in *Greater Love* by Michael Moynihan, 1980.

Letter from Percival Mundy *to* his father who lived in Bournemouth.
Lent by Mr. R. P. Whitehead (nephew).
Published: First published in this anthology.

Letter from Harry Waldo Yoxall, O.B.E., M.C., J.P. *to* his mother who lived in Kew, Surrey.
Lent by Mrs. Lindsey Pietrzak (daughter).
Published: First published in this anthology.

Letter from Edward Wyndham Tennant *to* his mother who lived at The Glen, Peebleshire, Scotland.
Lent by Lord Glenconnor (nephew).
Published: First published in this anthology.

Letter from John Parker *to* his brother-in-law who lived in South London.
Lent by Mrs. F. Davies (granddaughter).
Published: First published in this anthology.

Letter from Eric Marchant *to* his mother who lived in North London.
Lent by Miss Marjorie Marchant (sister).
Published: First published in this anthology.

Letter from John Coull *to* his son who lived in Aberdeen.
Lent by Mr. Frederick E. Coull (son).
Published: First published in this anthology.

Letter from Ernest Foster *to* Mr. and Mrs. Fairhead who lived in Norwich, Norfolk.
Lent by Mrs. Marjorie Potter (granddaughter of Mr. and Mrs. Fairhead).
Published: First published in this anthology.

Letter from James Milne *to* his wife who lived in Old Meldrum, Aberdeenshire.
Lent by Mr. William H. Milne (son).
Published: First published in this anthology.

Letter from Frank Orchard *to* his father who lived in Heathfield, Sussex.
Lent by Miss E. M. Orchard (sister).
Published: First published in this anthology.

Letter from William Murray *to* his father who lived in Longtown, Cumberland.
Lent by Miss Claudine Murray (sister).
Published: First published in this anthology.

Letter from Frederick Holman *to* his wife who lived in Hounslow, Middlesex.
Lent by Miss Joan Holman (daughter).
Published: First published in this anthology.

SECOND WORLD WAR

Poem 'Overseas' by Alan White.
Reprinted by permission of the Salamander Oasis Trust.

Published in *From Oasis Into Italy* by Victor Selwyn, Dan Davin, Erik Mauny and Ian Fletcher, 1983 Shepheard-Walwyn Publishers Ltd.

Letter from Edward Parry *to* his wife who lived in Uckfield, Sussex.
Lent by Miss Ann Parry (daughter).
Published: First published in this anthology.

Letter from Jack Toomey *to* his cousins.
Lent by Mrs. K. Toomey (widow).
Published: First published in this anthology.

Letter from John McComb, DFC, RAF, *to* his mother in Ribchester, near Preston, Lancashire.
Lent by Mrs. S. McComb (widow).
Published: First published in this anthology.

Letter from Leslie Carter *to* his mother who lived in Shenley, Hertfordshire.
Lent by Mrs Jeanetta Carter (mother).
Published: First published in this anthology.
Photograph of Leslie Carter kindly loaned by Mrs. Jeanetta Carter.

Letter from Eric Rafferty *to* his son who lived in Pimlico, London.
Lent by Mr. and Mrs. Eric Rafferty.
Published: First published in the *Daily Herald*, 1 May, 1944.
Photograph of Robert and Mrs. Rafferty kindly loaned by Mr. and Mrs. Eric Rafferty.

Letter from John Wyatt *to* his parents who lived in Sydenham, South London.
Lent by Mr. John Wyatt.
Published: First published in this anthology.

Letter from George Morrison *to* his mother.
Lent by Mrs. W. E. Reid (sister).
Published: First published in this anthology.

Letter from L. E. Stockwell *to* his wife who lived in Teddington, Middlesex.
Lent by Mrs. Gwenyth Stockwell (widow).
Published: First published in this anthology.
Photograph of L. E. Stockwell kindly loaned by Mrs. Gwenyth Stockwell.

Letter from Christopher Milner *to* his parents who lived in Kenilworth, Warwickshire.
Lent by Major Christopher Milner, M.C.
Published: First published in this anthology.
Photograph of General Montgomery kindly loaned by Major Christopher Milner.

Letter from Jack Yeoman *to* Stella O'Hare who lived in Liverpool.
Lent by Miss Stella O'Hare.
Published: First published in this anthology.

Photographs of Jack Yeoman and Stella O'Hare kindly loaned by Miss Stella O'Hare.

Letter from Edward Cope *to* Doreen Roots who lived in Morden, Surrey.
Lent by Mr. E. W. Cope.
Published: First published in this anthology.
Photograph of a letter from Edward Cope to Doreen Roots kindly loaned by Mr. E. W. Cope.

Letter from Lionel Wigram *to* his wife who lived at Merrow, Nr. Guildford, Surrey.
Lent by Mrs. Olga Wigram (widow).
Published: First published in this anthology.

Letters from Bill and John Smith *to* their parents who lived in Birkenhead, Cheshire.
Lent by Mr. Walter Smith (brother).
Published: First published in this anthology.

Letter from Lewis Bull *to* his family who lived in Brede, Sussex.
Lent by Mr. C. A. Bull (brother).
Published: First published in the *Sunday Pictorial*, 6 February, 1944.

Letter from John Harper-Nelson *to* his family who lived in Pimlico, London.
Lent by Mr. John Harper-Nelson.
Published: First published in this anthology.

Letter from Joseph Goodlad *to* his wife who lived in Bolton, Lancashire.
Lent by Mrs. Dorothy Goodlad (widow).
Published: First published in this anthology.
Photograph of Joseph Goodlad kindly loaned by Mrs. Dorothy Goodlad.

Letter from Gerald Ritchie *to* his sister who lived in North Yorkshire.
Lent by Major Gerald Ritchie, M.C.
Published: First published in this anthology.

Letter from Cedric Carryer *to* his mother who lived in Barkby, Leicestershire.
Lent by Mr. Cedric Carryer.
Published: First published in this anthology.

Letter from Ivor Rowbery *to* his mother who lived in Wolverhampton, in the Midlands.
Lent by Miss Patricia Rowbery (sister).
Published: First published in the *Tatler & Bystander*, 18 September, 1946.
Photograph of Ivor Rowbery kindly loaned by Miss Particia Rowbery.

Letter from George Leinster *to* his mother who lived in Whitley Bay, Northumberland.
Lent by Mrs. Patricia Leinster (widow).
Published: First published in this anthology.

Photograph of George Leinster kindly loaned by Mrs. Patricia Leinster.

Letter from Edward Hill-Heathcock *to* his neighbour Derek Watkins who lived in Stourbridge, in the Midlands.
Lent by Mr. Derek Watkins.
Published: First published in this anthology.

Letter from A. P. Reesberg *to* Gilbert Morgan's mother who lived in Redfield, Bristol.
Lent by Mrs. Grace Hodge (sister of Gilbert Morgan).
Published: First published in this anthology.
Photograph of Gilbert Morgan kindly loaned by Mrs. Grace Hodge.

Letter from Sam Carson *to* his family who lived in Glasgow, Scotland.
Lent by Mr. Sam Carson.
Published: First published in this anthology.

Letter from Peter Gadsdon *to* his parents who lived in Bognor Regis, Sussex.
Lent by Major Peter Gadsdon, M.B.E., M.C.
Published: First published in this anthology.

Letter from Bob Grafton *to* Dorothy who lived in Manor Park, East London.
Lent by Mr. Bob Grafton.
Published: First published in this anthology.

Photographs, Illustrations and Documents

Unless otherwise stated all photographs are reprinted by kind permission of the Imperial War Museum.

FIRST WORLD WAR

Photograph of a postcard from Edward Simpson *to* his wife.
Lent by Mrs. Winifred Armstrong (daughter). (Page 5.)

Photograph of a letter from George Hayman *to* his wife who lived in Manchester.
Lent by Mr. Max Hayman (son). (Page 46.)

Photograph of a drawing of Edward Wyndham Tennant.
Lent by Preston Manor House, Brighton. (Page 50.)

Photographs of stationery issued to the troops and censored envelopes.
Lent by Mrs. G. F. Ball. (Pages 42, 51.)

SECOND WORLD WAR

Photograph of an envelope and letter from G. F. Ball *to* his mother who lived in Birmingham.
Lent by Mr. G. F. Ball. (Page 75.)

Photographs of Air Graph Cards from Charles Thorley *to* his wife who lived in Wem, Shropshire.
Lent by Mrs. Kathleen Thorley (wife). (Pages 98–99.)

Photograph of a soldier with a letter he has just received from home.
Lent by Mr. H. W. Green. (Page 103.)

Photographs of postcards from Thomas Smithson *to* his wife who lived in Bolton, Lancashire.
Lent by Mr. Thomas Smithson. (Pages 104–105.)

Photograph of a drawing by Leonard Hughes *to* his wife.
Lent by Mr. Leonard Hughes. (Page 122.)